GIRL WITH A ROSE

A Tess Winnett
Novella

LESLIE WOLFE

PRAISE FOR *GIRL WITH A ROSE*

"Endless drama. Story and characters were well described. As always, a must read. Highly recommend. Ended too soon but I still loved it."

"I read this in one sitting! Kept me interested, the suspense and story line are well done. My first from this author but not my last!"

"Once you read the opening paragraph, you're hooked. Our heroine barely takes a breath as she searches for a missing teenager. You too will be holding you breath as you fly through the pages. I'm on to book 2."

"Very good .. Dark and detailed. Jumps right in and will leave you wanting more. I look forward to reading more books by her"

"Great and fast paced story! I was shocked that so much information was loaded into this short storyline, but still had great depth and characterizations!"

PRAISE FOR LESLIE WOLFE

"I'm so hooked on her books. I finish one and go straight to the next. They get you hooked from page one and the endings always have a twist."

"Really love the author. Her books are different and holds your attention.. I am anxious to read more"

"Suspenseful, intriguing and held my attention from page one. Ms Wolfe never cease to amaze me with her incredible stories."

"Leslie Wolfe always turns out a good read! Just enough twists and turns to keep you guessing and then then gob-smacked by the ending! Loved it."

"Leslie Wolfe always provides the reader with a suspenseful, page turning thriller! I continue to look forward to all of her new releases!"

BOOKS BY LESLIE WOLFE

STANDALONE TITLES

A Beautiful Couple
The Surgeon
The Girl You Killed
The Hospital
If I Go Missing
Stories Untold
Love, Lies and Murder

TESS WINNETT SERIES

Dawn Girl
The Watson Girl
Glimpse of Death
Taker of Lives
Not Really Dead
Girl With A Rose
Mile High Death
The Girl They Took
The Girl Hunter

DETECTIVE KAY SHARP SERIES

The Girl From Silent Lake
Beneath Blackwater River
The Angel Creek Girls
The Girl on Wildfire Ridge
Missing Girl at Frozen Falls

BAXTER & HOLT SERIES

Las Vegas Girl
Casino Girl
Las Vegas Crime

ALEX HOFFMANN SERIES

Executive
Devil's Move
The Backup Asset
The Ghost Pattern
Operation Sunset

For the complete list of books in all available formats, visit:
Amazon.com/LeslieWolfe

GIRL WITH A ROSE

A Tess Winnett
Novella

LESLIE WOLFE

$\mathllap{I\!I}$ **ITALICS**

Italics Publishing Inc.

Edited by Joni Wilson.
Cover and interior design by Sam Roman.

ACKNOWLEDGMENT

A special thank you to Mark Freyberg, my New York City authority for all matters legal. Mark's command of the law and passion for deciphering its intricacies translates into zero unanswered questions for this author. He's a true legal oracle and a wonderful friend.

1

POSE

She was thrilled she'd agreed to pose for him.

She almost hadn't made it past the imposing gates of the mansion, the likes of such she'd only seen in the movies. But the man had left a four-digit code scribbled with his address, and after fidgeting in place in front of the twelve-foot high, wrought-iron entrance, she noticed the keypad on a stand at the edge of the driveway, at the right height to be accessed from the driver's seat of a car. She'd entered the four digits with slightly trembling fingers, and the wrought iron set in motion, opening without a sound.

Mom would kill me if she knew where I'm at, she'd thought excitedly, her rebellion putting a spring in her step.

She'd walked the long, curvy driveway in a daze, taking in the beauty of the landscape with its fantastic rose bushes, each of them a different, exotic variety. She'd stopped a couple of times and buried her face in the dew-sprinkled blooms, taking in their aroma, savoring their intoxicating scent.

Then she rang the bell, while butterflies swarmed in her belly, and he opened the door almost immediately. He wore tight, worn-out jeans and a white T-shirt, both stained with paint, as were his arms and even his smiling face. She followed him inside, too intimidated to articulate a single word, her eyes riveted on the paintings that covered the walls of the living room. Beautiful girls, some sad, some playful, all young and innocent, their beauty enhanced by a single rose bloom.

Her step slowed and faltered as a strange sense of foreboding chilled her blood. She gazed quickly at the paintings again, this time searching the girls' eyes, looking for something, for a clue into what was to come, but their expressions remained mysterious, almost grim. The chill in her body turned to icicles streaming in her blood, and she let a quiet whimper escape her lips.

He turned and smiled, his smile warming the room. "What's wrong, my dear?"

She felt like an idiot. Posing for such an artist was a huge opportunity for her, and she was screwing it up as only she could. "Um, nothing, really," she managed, wringing her hands nervously and avoiding his deep, blue eyes. "All this," she gestured toward the walls covered in luxuriously framed canvases, "I—I don't know what to say."

"They're beautiful, aren't they?" he said, his voice filled with warmth as if the girls immortalized on canvas were all long-departed friends he dearly missed.

Then he turned toward her and widened his smile. "But they're gone… and you're here. You're even more beautiful, Kaylee."

Blood rushed to her cheeks, warming them quickly.

"When we're finished, I'll make room for you right here, above the mantle. You'll be my *pièce de résistance*," he added, the French words lending their charm to his already charismatic voice. His fingers brushed against her cheek for an instant, in a featherlight touch. "Your beauty is unique."

The last shadow of foreboding coldness left her body under his electrifying touch. She smiled timidly, painfully aware of how out of place she looked, of how childish her behavior was. She desperately wished she could instantly be a few years older and the kind of girl this man could fall in love with.

And she didn't even know his name.

She breathed and decided the woman he would like for more than a model for a painting would have the courage to ask his name.

"What, um, do I call you?" she managed, blushing again at the sound of her voice, strangled by emotion.

"David," he replied, searching her eyes and still smiling. "You can call me David." Then he turned to leave, looking at her over his shoulder. "Come on, we've got work to do, and we'll lose the light in a few hours."

She followed him eagerly through another couple of rooms, then entered his studio. An entire wall was made of glass panels, letting the sunshine in without restrictions. Through the large windows, she could see the exquisite garden in the back of the house, intricate alleys weaving between rose beds with blooms in various colors and shapes. Here and there, wooden benches under the shade of secular oaks or a fountain springing crystalline water on top of carefully arranged boulders.

It was as if she'd left the modern age at the wrought-iron gate and had entered the mansion of a nineteenth-century royal.

Surreal.

And it would make one hell of a story to tell Alice tomorrow. She'd have to share some of her adventures with her best friend, in return for her commitment to cover for Kaylee at school and with her mother, in case things would run late here and she'd call, all freaked out like Mom always got when she was even a minute past her curfew. School was easy, knowing how the Catholic prudes rushed to change the subject when any mention of cramps or other period-related issues were brought up, especially by a freshman. But her mom was another thing altogether; no mention of cramps would fly with her. *Being a teenager sucks*, she thought bitterly. *All day in school, then rushing home or else Mom throws a fit and grounds me forever, when I could be hanging out here, with a guy like that.*

"Don't," David said gently, touching her chin briefly to invite her to look at him.

"Huh?" she reacted, taken by surprise.

"You're frowning," he said, a tinge of disappointment in his voice.

She smiled apologetically and looked around for a place to sit.

There were a few pieces of furniture in the studio, scattered loosely on the vast floor in front of an easel holding a large canvas, all upholstered in black leather. A large armchair Kaylee could've easily curled up in, with her legs folded under her, and taken a nap. An inviting lounge chair that looked cozy and comfortable, the kind she'd seen only in fashion magazines. A bed, covered in red satin sheets and littered with pillows of all colors, the sight of which brought fire to her face. And a wide bench without a backrest, long enough to seat three, maybe four, people.

A new smile tugged at the corners of David's mouth as he followed her gaze.

"Let's seat you over here," he said, pointing at the bench.

She obeyed and sat, amazed at the softness of the leather under her touch.

"I brought some different clothes," she said, taking off her backpack.

"No need," he replied, his smile gone, replaced with an intense, scrutinizing look.

Her frown returned promptly. "You're painting me in my school clothes?" Her disappointment was raw, carrying the promise of tears.

"No, my dear," he replied, almost absentmindedly, ambling around her, studying her in detail. "This will be a head portrait."

"Oh," she whispered, feeling intimidated again under his scrutiny. Was her skin perfect? How about her hair?

"Did you remember to turn off your cell phone, like I asked? I don't like being interrupted while I work."

"Yes," she replied quickly, pulling it out of her pocket and showing him the dark screen.

"Good," he replied, then moved the easel a few feet to the right. He peeked from behind the canvas to look at her and then disappeared again for a few moments.

She heard his footsteps leaving the room, but she stayed in place, unsure of what to do. In his absence, the sense of foreboding returned, chilling her blood once again. There was a half-finished canvas leaned against the wall, the portrait of a girl holding a rose blossom to her lips, but her eyes looked haunted as if life was leaving her body. Kaylee's skin prickled with goosebumps, and she wrapped her arms around herself, shivering.

"It gets cold in here in the mornings," David said, startling her. She'd not heard him return, but he was there by her side, holding a steaming cup of tea. "The studio doesn't have heating, but the sun will do the trick." He offered her the cup. "It's chamomile with a touch of honey; it will help you relax."

She took the cup and, under his commanding gaze, took a sip. It was delicious, warming her body and scaring the apprehension away. She thanked him and sipped again, letting the thin vapor touch her face.

He walked over to a small table and brought back a tray, setting it on the bench by her side. Laid neatly on the tray were hairbrushes and combs, several fancy hairpins and accessories, scissors, and a few rose blooms in different shades of pink.

"May I?" he asked, picking up a hairbrush.

She shrugged. "Sure." She bit her lip, trying to hide her nervousness at the thought of him touching her. Yet strangely, she was disappointed he'd chosen pink blooms for her when the garden held stunning shades of crimson, purple, even blue with a yellow center. Pink was so banal.

He was gentle, removing her scrunchy without pulling her hair. Then he brushed it until it crackled with electricity, stopping a few times to evaluate the results of his work. Kaylee wished there was a mirror in the room, where she could see what she would look like after he was finished. She'd probably have to wait for the painting to be done to see her new image.

He set the hairbrush down and whispered, "Good." Then he lifted her hair up, strand by strand, weaving and arranging it in a high, braided updo pinned in place with a sophisticated, diamond-encrusted clip. Then he loosened a few thin strands around her face and arranged them carefully with his fingers, his face so close to hers she could feel his breath on her cheeks, sending shivers through her body.

He took a few steps back to admire his work, then let a quiet whistle sum up his conclusions.

She smiled widely. "Is there a mirror—"

His frown returned, digging deep ridges in his forehead. "No mirror, no. Please, be patient."

She lowered her gaze and took another sip of tea, a touch of uneasiness unfurling in her gut, a feeling she couldn't name, a warning she couldn't read.

He picked up a rose, then removed all its thorns with a pair of scissors. He trimmed the stem to four or five inches, then slid the stem behind her ear and secured the heavy bloom in place with two hair clips.

"We're ready," David said, rubbing his hands together, satisfied. "Finish your tea so we can get started."

She was happy to oblige, her throat feeling parched for some reason. She felt weak, almost trembling, and hoped the honey in the tea would pick her up a little and give her a touch of a sugar rush.

She set the empty cup on the bench near her, seeing more than feeling how badly her hand shook. His eyes lingered on her trembling hand, but he said nothing. He disappeared behind the canvas for a few moments and returned pushing a small cart with paint tubes, a small bowl, and a makeup kit like she'd never seen before. Only artists and musicians must've had a case like that, a silver suitcase that arranged in three levels when open, holding everything she could ever need if she were a star.

Dizzy and a little nauseated, she took her frozen hand to her forehead, hoping that the cold touch would make her feel better.

"Don't touch your hair," David commanded, his voice strong, almost angry.

She let her hand fall back into her lap. She tried to speak, but only a faint whimper came out. "I—I can't—"

"Here, lie down," he invited, supporting her head carefully with his hand until it touched the soft cushion of the bench. He slid a pillow under her head, then put her legs up on the bench with gentle, thoughtful moves.

He wasn't asking the right questions, wasn't calling an

ambulance. Her prior sense of foreboding had returned as sheer panic, but she couldn't scream, she couldn't move. She could still focus her eyes somewhat and watched every move he made while terror took over her heart, knowing what he'd done when he'd spiked her tea, but not understanding why.

"You must feel dizzy and numb right now," he explained patiently as if talking to a small child, "and that's normal. Well, maybe not to you, but I can assure you it's quite normal to me." He caressed her cheek, removing a rebel strand of thin, blonde hair. "I know you'd like me to say that everything will be all right, and it will be, but not for you, my dear. Not for you. Although you might enjoy what's coming."

He picked up a small porcelain bowl and held it above her face. "Do you know what this is? Bone ash porcelain. Human bones, burned to ash, are mixed in with the kaolin, to make the finest pieces of china there can be. The bones make the material stronger so that the porcelain can be thinner, almost translucent. See?"

She couldn't say a word. She tried, but no sound came out of her mouth, as panicked thoughts raced through her mind. What time was it? When would her mom freak out and call someone? A tear rolled down her cheek and disappeared in her hair. *Mom,* she called in her mind, *please find me. I promise I'll be good. I'll never lie to you again.*

She felt a pinprick in her arm and watched as David pierced her vein with a thin needle attached to a small plastic tube. Unable to lift her head, she could barely see what he was doing, but he'd elevated her arm on a couple of pillows, and she could catch a foggy glimpse.

Her blurry eyes locked on the blood leaving her body, in a steady string of droplets, collecting in the bone china bowl engraved with intricate gold leaves. She drew breath and let out a shriek that no one heard, not even her; no sound came off her parted lips.

He grinned and wiped her tears with cold fingers. "You mustn't cry, my dear. I'll apply your makeup next, and you're going to ruin it all."

Her heart fluttered frantically against her rib cage like a trapped bird fighting for its life, willing to smash itself against the bars rather than die at the hand of its captor. But all she could do was watch every move he made, unable to fight, unable to resist.

He mixed a few droplets of blood with paint from various tubes, adjusting the composition until it seemed perfect to him. Then he applied the paint on her lips, checking the crimson hue against direct sunlight and shade. He added a few droplets to some scrapings of eyeshadow on a tiny plate stained with dried paint, tinting the powder's hue to match the lipstick. She felt the applicator touch her eyelids gently, while his finger forced her eyes shut, one at a time.

"That's it," he exclaimed happily. "You're ready, my dear, and you are absolutely exquisite." He chuckled lightly, but then groaned and rushed to tap her cheek with a napkin. "No more crying, you hear me? You'll ruin everything."

He stared at her and licked his lips with anticipation, his charismatic smile turning into a grin filled with lust. He removed her clothing with ease, careful not to pull the needle out of her arm, then gave her young body one more appreciative look.

She tried to scream again; her desperate efforts, visible only in her eyes, bringing a lascivious smirk on his face.

"Scream all you want, my dear. I like you more when you're

feisty."

2
MISSING

Tess typed her report quickly, a faint smile lingering on her lips. Only one feeling was more rewarding than the closing of a case with a neatly typed final report, all t's crossed and all i's dotted: when she actually caught her man. Or woman, for that matter, but most of the unsubs were men. That unique, adrenaline-injecting moment that made her blood rush through her veins while her heart thumped loudly in her chest, when she had the unsub in her sights, exposed, cornered, finished. What a rush!

Unfortunately, that moment had also proved to be the one when most chose to forge ahead against all logic and leave her no other option but to discharge her weapon. Her smile vanished as she typed that section of the report, while the words of her supervisor, Special Agent in Charge Pearson, resounded in her memory.

"You have the highest kill rate in the entire regional bureau, Winnett," he'd said. "You've been cleared in every incident, but you're under scrutiny, and all your future cases will be reviewed by the committee. For a while, at least, until you demonstrate you can actually slap a pair of handcuffs on a perp and give the Miami-Dade State attorney a reason to earn his keep."

SAC Pearson would probably be *thrilled* to read her latest report, just as she was to write it, early in the morning, way before the office floor got busy with traffic and loud with chatter and phones ringing. Her latest case had involved a drug-smuggling ring that had expanded into human trafficking, and she'd caught the ringleader in the act. She should've waited and called for backup, but there was a chance the girls he and his cronies were escorting off a powerboat would disappear into the ring's maze of safe houses and brothels, never to be seen again. Out of options, she'd pulled out her weapon and summoned him to surrender, silently begging him to surrender quietly. He'd grinned and lunged at her, gun drawn, and she'd tapped him in the chest. Twice.

She'd managed to arrest the two other perps, but still.

SAC Pearson must've been already fuming. She could feel it in the air, in the deathly silence engulfing the entire floor, in the sideways glances the few early risers threw her way when passing by her desk. SACs were the first notified whenever a weapon was discharged by one of their agents. He must've been already rapping his fingers against the desk, awaiting her report, growing angrier by the minute. He was there... she didn't imagine things. The light was on in his office, and the door wide open. Oh, well. *Que será, será.*

She nodded slowly while rereading her report, editing a word here and there. Her eyes lingered for a moment on the document's header.

FBI Case Report by SSA Tess Winnett

She'd recently earned a promotion, adding the second "S" to the acronym preceding her name. Now she was a supervisory special agent with the Federal Bureau of Investigation. A supervisory without a team. An SSA who'd probably never get a team assigned to her, and she was grateful for that. She loved her job just the way it was: a primal manhunt, twisted mind games played with the most chilling murderers out there, unencumbered by the complication of working with others. Teamwork had never been her strength. She loved the pursuit of justice, the ability to right the ugliest and most twisted, perverted, and sickening wrongs in her corner of the world. Each solved case filled her chest with swelling pride, even if at times chilled by the anticipation of SAC Pearson's reprimand because this time, yet again, her main perp was hosted in the morgue, not in lockup.

Her phone rang, and she was startled, then groaned as she read the name on the caller ID, right underneath the time stamp showing 6:43 A.M. in digital script.

"In my office, Winnett," Pearson said, without giving her the time to say anything. "Now."

She swore under her breath and hit the print command on her keyboard, then paced around the printer like a caged animal, impatient to see all twelve pages come out of the machine. Then she grabbed them and the case folder and rushed out toward Pearson's office, without taking the time to arrange the pages and staple them together.

She found Pearson looking out the window with a sad expression on his face, and before he beckoned her in, she caught a glimpse of a black-and-white photo on his desk. It showed a much younger, slimmer Pearson, who still had hair on his head and knew how to smile, by the side of a determined, athletic woman, probably another FBI agent.

Tess handed Pearson the case file, but he gestured toward the pile on his desk and then invited her to take a seat.

"There's a missing persons case I'd like you to look into," he said, his eyes still riveted to the cityscape visible outside his window.

"Sure," she replied, wondering which miracles had aligned to work in her favor and help her skip past the chewing out she'd been expecting.

"It's a kid," he added with a barely contained sigh. "A fifteen-year-old girl."

"Fifteen?" she reacted. The FBI usually investigated missing or kidnapped children age twelve or younger, and there was a specialized response team for that, the Child Abduction Rapid Deployment Team, or CARD. When a fifteen-year-old went missing, there usually had to be local police involvement and a request for assistance was expected before the bureau would engage. "Which county called us in?"

Pearson hesitated for a split second, enough time for his expression to shift slightly, becoming more focused. He turned and looked straight at her.

"Do this as a personal favor to me, Winnett, will you?" He sounded pained, worried.

"Sure," she replied. "I'll need some details to get started." She took a small notebook out of her pocket and grabbed a pen from his desk.

He sat behind the desk, the chair grumbling under his massive frame. He stared for a moment at the photo of his younger self and the unknown woman, then rubbed his forehead as if fighting a silent migraine.

When he finally spoke, his tone was the one Tess knew well: firm, uncompromising, factual.

"Kaylee Lewis, fifteen, was last seen yesterday evening, when she left her friend's house, heading home. Both girls go to school at Bayshore High."

Tess whistled. That was one of the most expensive private schools in the area.

"There's a catch, Winnett," he added. "The last person to see Kaylee was Alice, her best friend. Alice Bachert is her full name."

Tess sprung to her feet. "The governor's kid?"

"Yes," Pearson said. "Sit down, Winnett."

"Are you setting me up, sir?" she asked, before she could realize what she was saying and to whom.

"Jeez, Winnett! Are you serious right now?"

"The governor asked you twice to get rid of me," she replied quickly, feeling the blood rush to her head. "Do you think I can waltz into his house and question his daughter?"

"Yes. You're the only one who can."

That answer left her slack-jawed and at a loss for words. She sat and waited for Pearson to say more.

"Bachert called me twice about you, in each case demanding your badge for bothering his friends. But you didn't care. You still closed those investigations successfully, while most agents would've considered the impact an enemy like the pissed-off governor of the state of Florida could've had on their careers."

"Oh, I see," she replied. "I'm now officially qualified fodder for the governor's shitfits," she mumbled.

"No, Winnett. You're the only agent in this regional office with a one hundred percent case close ratio. You have an open position waiting for you with Behavioral Analysis in Quantico that you refuse to accept, but it's still kept open, nevertheless. You're the best agent I can think of, the only one I trust with Kaylee's life. You don't care about politics and will bring Kaylee back to her mother at any cost."

"What about Bachert? He had it in for me when it was only about his friends being bothered with a few questions. Do you think sending me to his house to speak with his own kid is the best approach? This can go wrong in any number of different ways."

Pearson sighed, his patience running to a visible low. "Yeah, he'll call, and he'll complain, and he'll demand we fire you like he's done before. That doesn't mean we'll do that. Give us some credit, will you?"

She wasn't going to give *them* much credit, whoever *they* were. Maybe she'd give Pearson some credit, yes, considering he could've already fired her but had obviously decided against it. However, in her many years with the bureau, she'd seen politics in action before, turning friends into enemies and honest agents into backstabbers for far less. However, all Bacherts of the world aside, there was a kid missing, albeit for only a few hours. Screw that short-fused, entitled asshole.

"You could also choose to go easy on him, be polite, respectful, show some courtesy instead of your typical bluntness," Pearson added.

She frowned and glared but managed to refrain from adding she wasn't going to kiss a politician's rear end just to make him or Pearson happy.

"Let's talk about Kaylee," she replied instead. "Are we sure this kid didn't choose to go on a date that went a little long? Did the county log in her case as a missing person?" she asked, although she knew the answer. Police don't log a missing person's report in the first hours since they were last seen, it's usually after twenty-four hours.

"The mother called the police last night about eleven, but they haven't started an official investigation yet, and haven't called us in," he replied. He pushed the photo toward her and tapped his finger against its weathered surface. "Jennifer was my partner. An excellent agent, who taught me a lot of what I know today. Kaylee's mom is Jennifer's younger sister, Deanne. And Kaylee is my godchild," he added with a sad smile.

Tess wondered where the sadness was coming from. Kaylee

had barely gone missing, if she even was. Statistically, there was a good chance the girl would soon show up at home, begging her mother for forgiveness and swearing she'd never do it again. "How come Jennifer's not looking into this?"

"She was killed in the line of duty, almost ten years ago, in the same shootout that killed Kaylee's father. He was DEA."

"Oh," Tess whispered. She couldn't begin to imagine what Deanne and her daughter must've gone through that day, having to bury not one, but two loved ones. "Then we'll look into this ourselves. Why does her mother believe she's missing, as opposed to being inexcusably late?"

"Deanne called everyone she could think of, and no one has heard from her daughter after she left the Bachert residence about six. No texts, no Facebook, nothing. And she told me Kaylee's been different lately. New habits, new music, new clothes."

"Also known as being a teenager," Tess replied.

"That was my reaction too, but then Deanne said something I had to take seriously. She said she had a strong gut feeling about this."

"A parent's anxiety? That's all we have?"

"Kaylee's phone is off, and she's never broken the dusk curfew before." Pearson stopped for a moment, probably considering how unrealistic and thin his arguments were. "Kaylee's a good kid, Winnett. It's not like her to just vanish."

"A teenager with a dusk curfew?" She tried to refrain a smile. "How long was that going to last?"

"Okay, Winnett, you don't trust Deanne's gut. She's someone you've never met, in your mind just a scared, frantic parent fearing the worst. But do you trust *my* gut?"

Her smile vanished, and the answer came easily to her.

"With my life." In almost twelve years of working with him, Pearson had never been wrong. Not even once.

"Then believe me when I say, this girl's missing. She could've been taken, or just... something could've happened to her. This is Miami, Winnett, not a midwestern town where no one ever locks their doors."

"All right, that's good enough for me," she replied. "I'm assuming no ransom calls have been made yet?"

"None."

"I'll handle this angle too, just in case." She paused, checking her notes. "Deanne is a single mother, yet Kaylee is enrolled at a very expensive school. Is everything above water there?" She saw Pearson's frown and added, "I mean no disrespect. But if we have gang activity here, or some drug connection, I need to know."

"Deanne is a dentist with her own practice. I also happen to know that Kaylee's tuition is covered by her paternal grandparents, both retired attorneys."

Tess flipped the notebook shut. "That explains it," then checked her watch briefly. "She's been missing a little over twelve hours. We're still in the first twenty-four, but I'll drop everything and head out straight for the lion's lair."

"Huh?" Pearson reacted, looking up from Tess's latest case file.

"My good old friend, the governor. I'm heading out there now. I want to catch everyone while they're still at home. Expect your phone to start ringing. The man just hates my guts."

She stood, while Pearson looked at her intently, irritated at first, then almost pleading.

"For heaven's sake, Winnett, a kid's missing, do your damn

job already."

Offended, she took a couple of steps back. "Of course, I'll do my job; just saying there will be damage control left for you to clean up, sir."

Pearson glared at her without a word.

She turned and walked briskly out of his office, then shouted from the hallway, "And I'll need Donovan."

3

A ROSE

Tess checked the time as she rushed toward Donovan's desk. He'd just arrived and was setting up for his day at the office. A large, transparent plastic travel mug with water and floating pieces of fruit came out of his backpack and landed on a coaster next to his keyboard. He held a smaller, paper cup, filled with coffee to the brim, taking small sips every second or so, while he fired up his computers.

An amazing analyst and a frustrated professional at the same time, Donovan tried every year for field agent and was rejected, also every year. The reason remained a mystery, at least for Tess. She'd probed with Pearson a couple of times, but he'd cut her curiosity off without disclosing any information. It could've been because the tall, broad-shouldered man lacked some critical skill needed in the field, or because he was so darn good at what he did that the regional bureau couldn't begin to imagine the workplace without Donovan as a technical analyst.

"Ah, the highlight of my day has just materialized," Donovan said in lieu of a greeting.

Or it could've been his manners. Cynical, dismissive at times, rushed, and usually sarcastic, coming across as arrogant to the bone, Donovan bristled almost everyone he worked with.

"Good morning to you too," Tess replied, unfazed. "We have an urgent missing persons case I need your—"

"Pearson's mystery kid?"

"It's not his kid, D, it's his godchild," she sighed. "And yes.

Her name is Kaylee Lewis."

Donovan's monitors were all lit up. He abandoned the coffee cup with a regretful look and sat in front of them, ready to type.

"Tell me what you need."

"I need ransom call and tracing deployed at the Lewis residence."

His fingers still lingered, immobile, above the keyboard.

"Done. I wasn't the only one Pearson woke up before the alarm clock."

She didn't bother to set him straight but felt a pang of frustration that her boss had called her analyst before he'd called her.

"Did you run a trace on the girl's phone?"

"The phone's off and hasn't pinged the network since yesterday at 12:37 P.M. Still waiting to hear back on the last known location."

She checked the time again and groaned.

"Too late now to rush to the governor's house. I'll interview Kaylee's mother first, then her best friend." She frowned as she considered her options. "Could you please call the Bachert residence and let them know I'm coming? I'll need Alice to be available to answer questions about Kaylee."

"Nice, Winnett," he grinned with clenched teeth. "Use me to handle that hot potato."

"He won't say anything to you," she replied. "He'll save it all for me."

She drove with lights and siren on to the Lewis residence, wondering why the girl had turned off her phone in the middle of a school day. Most kids spent their entire lunch breaks with their faces buried in the devices, preferring to text their friends instead of actually speaking with them, even if they're seated at the same table.

She found the residence easily. It was the only house on the quiet Bayshore street with three black SUVs parked in front, all with government plates. She recognized a couple of technicians from the bureau and greeted them, getting out of their way as they hauled call tracking and recording equipment. Within minutes, the technicians finished setting up, and two of the SUVs drove away, leaving behind a junior agent by the name of Gabriel Mendoza to pace the dimly lit living room with a wireless headset around his neck, waiting for the ransom call.

"Hey, Mendoza," she greeted him in a low whisper. "Where's—?"

He gestured with his head and she followed the direction of his glance. Deanne sat in the corner of the couch, crying softly. She must've sensed Tess approaching, because she looked up, then sprung to her feet.

"Have you heard anything?" she asked Tess, wiping her tears with the back of her hand.

"Nothing yet," Tess replied, and her two words sent a shockwave through the woman's body.

She sat, her feet seemingly too weak to sustain her.

"I have a few questions for you," Tess said. "Tell me about Kaylee. What's she like?"

"She's a wonderful kid," Deanne replied. "It's been just the two of us since her dad died, and she's strong and sweet, a good student." She sniffled, then looked at Tess with pleading eyes. "This isn't like her, to just disappear. You have to believe me. She'd never do that to me."

"I understand," Tess replied. The woman had given her almost zero useful information. Who was Kaylee as a person? Sometimes parents are the last to know when their children grow up and become individuals with entirely different, secret lives.

"Tell me about her friends." She decided to take a structured approach to the interview. "Who does she spend her time with?"

"Alice. Everything Kaylee does is with Alice, and I couldn't be happier about it. Alice is a nice girl, and her family is, well, the governor's family, so Kaylee spends a lot of time at their house. I know she's safe there. They study together, go to camp together, they've been inseparable since they were little," Deanne said, putting her hand in the air about three feet from the ground.

"Anyone else? Is there a boyfriend?"

"There is, or was, I should say," Deanne replied hesitantly. "Kaylee went out a couple of times with this boy from school, Jeremy Gafford. But now that you asked, I realize she hasn't been talking about him much lately. She tells me everything, my little girl," Deanne added, wiping a fresh tear off her cheek. "My days are long at the clinic, but dinners are a sacred ritual for my daughter and me. We talk about our day, laugh a little, and I try hard not to ask too much about schoolwork. She's an A student, you know."

Tess repressed a frustrated groan. She'd seen it many times before, when parents couldn't provide much insight into their children's interests and routine.

"How about her phone? Do you check your daughter's social media and texts?"

"Um, no... I respect her privacy and give her some freedom, more each year," Deanne replied, a hint of worry in her eyes.

For a brief moment, Tess considered whether to tell Deanne how wrong that was, in a world filled with psychopaths and pedophiles preying on children through social media. Maybe it wasn't the right moment to seed more fear in the poor woman's heart.

"What does Kaylee like?" she asked instead.

Deanne's face lit up. "She's into fashion a lot, always watching fashion shows and following supermodels on the internet. She is very particular about her looks, almost a little vain," she added, her voice tinged with guilt. "She accessorizes better than I do, and picks my own attire, because I'm just too busy to care much these days."

The statement rang true; Deanne wore simple, beige slacks and a white shirt.

She stood and invited Tess to follow her to the hallway, where framed photos showed Kaylee at various ages, always perfectly dressed, smiling with perfectly aligned, white teeth, her makeup impeccable.

Deanne being a dentist, the perfect dentition was to be expected. But the makeup? What age did teenage girls start using makeup these days?

"May I see her room?" Tess asked, and Deanne led the way.

Kaylee's bedroom was nothing Tess expected. Where teenagers lived, there usually was clutter, as if tornadoes routinely swirled everything in the air and then let objects fall to the ground where they happened to land. Kaylee's room was neat, the bed made impeccably with throw pillows arranged symmetrically and a plush teddy bear leaning against the middle pillow. Not a single sock, shoe, or clothing item lay scattered anywhere in sight. Curious, Tess opened the closet and found the same rigorous order ruling the countless clothes hangers and folded items.

Kaylee's room seemed ready for a fashion magazine layout

shoot. The rest of the house, however, seemed lived in.

"Who makes the bed?" Tess asked. "Do you have a housekeeper?"

"We have a service that comes every two weeks for major cleaning," Deanne said, sounding embarrassed. Probably, in the ritzy Bayshore area, it was inconceivable not to have a full-time maid. "But no, Kaylee makes her bed like that, every morning. And cleans up perfectly."

Tess frowned, but chose not to ask Deanne if she thought that behavior was normal for a teenager.

"She wants everything to be perfect," Deanne explained, understanding Tess's unspoken question. "She's a little vain, you know. I believe she might be competing with Alice somehow. You know, the governor has three permanent house staff, and everything is perfect in their household. Probably Kaylee doesn't want to be embarrassed when Alice visits."

"Makes sense," Tess conceded, although it didn't. Not really.

She opened a few desk drawers and examined the items neatly organized. Writing instruments in one, books and notepads in another. Then she went to the closet again and started opening drawers. At the far end of a sock drawer, she found an Estée Lauder makeup kit that must've been expensive. She pulled it out and opened it, while Deanne stared at it in disbelief.

"I didn't know she had this," she whispered. "I sometimes put a bit of makeup on her when we're going out or something. But I thought—" Her words trailed off as she covered her mouth with her hand.

"Most girls hide their makeup," Tess replied, studying Kaylee's clothing closely. Some of the items were expensive, but not beyond what a dentist mom could afford. "You bought her all these clothes?"

Deanne looked at the stacked closet closely. "Um, I recognize most of them, so, yes, I believe I did. Some are hand-me-downs, clothes I used to wear when I was younger."

Tess slid the closet door shut and returned near the bed. A couple of magazines were laid on the night table, again an unusual choice for a girl Kaylee's age. *American Art* and *Artists*, both recent issues and both showing signs of repeated use.

"Is Kaylee into art?" Tess asked, looking at the walls decorated with the typical band posters that teenagers liked. There was no art; Kaylee was a fan of Twenty One Pilots and Imagine Dragons.

"Not until recently," Deanne replied, frowning impatiently when Tess sat on the edge of the bed with the latest issue of *American Art* open in her lap.

Tess flipped through the pages carefully, wondering what Kaylee's interest could've been. Her interest must've been major, because the subscription, per the discount coupon included in the magazine's pages, was not cheap.

The pages gave off a fine scent, a whiff of high-end cologne, or some other scented cosmetic. She closed her eyes and inhaled, trying to identify the mysterious smell. Shower gel, maybe? *No, it's aftershave*, she concluded silently. That magazine did not come straight from the newsstand.

"Do you really have time for this?" Deanne snapped, her voice angry, her eyes filled with tears.

Tess stood, abandoning the magazine on the bed. "My only chance to find your daughter and bring her back to you is to understand who she is, what makes her tick."

Deanne shook her head. "I already told you…"

"Who is she, really? How would a predator approach her?

What would he lure her with? If she's a little vain and into fashion, would someone offer her a modeling audition?"

Deanne wailed, bending over with her hands clutched at her chest, as if the cry ripped her apart.

Great work, Winnett, always ready to put your foot in your mouth, Tess admonished herself for her bluntness.

She gently touched Deanne's shoulder.

"I promise you, I'll do everything in my power to find your daughter. And I'm not alone. I have resources, Pearson and the entire team are behind this investigation and we're not stopping until we find her."

Deanne straightened her back and looked Tess straight in the eye. "Find my baby... please. I—I can't think that someone took her... has her. I just... can't."

Kaylee had been gone more than twelve hours, and the absence of a ransom call was a bad sign. She could've been anywhere... snatched off the streets of Miami by human traffickers, to be shipped to who knows where and forced into prostitution. She'd just put a human trafficking ringleader into the ground, but probably by now three more had taken his place.

Kaylee could've been grabbed at random by a predator or lured by a stalker. She could've been attacked in the street and left bleeding in some alley. Regardless of the scenario, Kaylee's time was running out fast. The first twenty-four hours were critical; after that, the chances of finding a missing person alive plummeted, and the most likely scenario would be finding her body. Those were the odds. If Alice had told the truth, Kaylee had last been seen at six P.M. the night before; almost fifteen hours.

Instead of sharing her thoughts, Tess held the woman's gaze

with a determined, reassuring look. "I promise," she replied. "Kaylee's one of ours, and we *will* find her."

Tess turned to leave, but another object caught her eye. A single, long-stemmed rose in perfect pink bloom, in a thin crystal vase, arranged tastefully at the center of a dresser. Not the usual fifteen-year-old bedroom décor.

"When's her birthday?" Tess asked.

"Kaylee turned fifteen almost a month ago."

"And this?" Tess pointed at the rose. "Secret admirer?"

A faint, sad smile fluttered on Deanne's lips. "She's not like that, I wish you'd believe me. No... this came from her best friend, Alice. She does these things sometimes."

Alice again.

4

MESSAGE

From the Lewis residence to the governor's, the drive was short, albeit through tourist-jammed traffic despite the early hour. Cursing under her breath, she speed-dialed Donovan's phone.

"Shoot," he answered. She could hear him typing on his keyboard in short, rapid bursts.

"I confirmed Kaylee only had the one cell phone," Tess said. "Any—"

"I have the last location it pinged, and it's not where you'd expect." Donovan paused, whistling rhythmically to voice his impatience. "Okay, got it. Kaylee lives in Bayshore, and the school is south of her address, by the Botanical Garden. The governor lives a mile north of there, on Pine Tree, by the park. So, you'd expect the phone to have pinged its swan song somewhere between those points, the governor's house as the north boundary of the area, and the school as the south, with Biscayne Bay and Indian Creek as the west and east boundaries, respectively."

"Okay, where did the phone ping last?"

"In North Beach. It's at least five miles north of where she should've been at 12:37 P.M."

"At that time, she should've been in school," Tess said, more to herself. "Can you track this phone's location for, say, two weeks? Let's find out where she's been hanging out."

"It will take some doing," Donovan mumbled, typing quickly.

"Only if you can," she added, feeling a tad guilty for pressing his buttons like that, but she was desperate for time.

"Of course, I can," he replied, sounding offended. "I'll do the same for Alice's phone, to see where and when they were together."

"You have her number?" There was no limit to the man's ingenuity. Maybe his ego was inflated for good reason.

"I have all the numbers registered on the governor's account, and only one pings in Bayshore High every day. I'm guessing that's not Mr. Almighty Bachert himself, going through puberty again."

"How about Kaylee's social media accounts? Did you manage—?"

"Her passwords were simple, as expected. Skimming through them now, just give me a moment."

"Do you see any art postings? Anything art related?"

"Art? No, nothing. Just the typical teenager stuff. Music, funny memes, some sexual innuendo, and an absolutely horrendous number of selfies. I'm so ready for facial recognition to work as well as it should..." His voice trailed off, while he probably scrolled through Kaylee's profile pages. "A couple of cat videos, and a ton of Messenger exchanges with Alice."

Tess groaned, while pulling in at the curb in front of the governor's house, the last residence before the park. The property was entirely shielded from view by rows of thick palm trees and shrubs lining with green a masonry fence interrupted by a wrought-iron gate that was wide open, probably in anticipation of her arrival.

"Here's something interesting, listen to this," Donovan said, just as she was about to cut the engine. "Two nights ago,

Kaylee said, in a private message to Alice, 'I'm falling in love... I'd go anywhere for him, do anything for him.' There's a man involved, Tess."

There always was. And he'd left his scent in Kaylee's room.

"Did Alice reply in any way?"

"N—nah... she definitely didn't ask her who she was talking about. Alice knows who the man is. I'll go back a few gazillion messages to see if I can find anything."

Tess ended the call and cut the engine, then let out a long sigh. She had to tread lightly, but all leads led to Alice, probably the only Florida resident Tess couldn't hope to interview without interference.

Darn Alice again.

5

STANDOFF

Tess rang the bell at the governor's house and pulled out her badge, ready to present it to the person who opened the door. Instead, the governor himself greeted her with a scowl and a frown that dug deep into his brow. He was wearing one of the charcoal suits with a white shirt and silk tie that she'd seen him wear routinely in his almost daily TV interviews. But the smile he usually reserved for the media was absent. His gaze was threatening, uncompromising, part of the fierceness in it reminiscent of the years he'd spent distinguishing himself as a Marine sniper. At almost sixty years old, Governor Bachert seemed just as fearless and steeled as the young sniper might've been, but only stronger, bolder. More dangerous.

"I would've expected you to show up sooner, Agent Winnett," he said, then stepped to the side to allow her to come in. "I thought this was an urgent matter."

"I can assure you it is," Tess replied, sustaining his gaze unperturbed. "A teenage girl you know personally has gone missing, and the last person to see her before she disappeared was your daughter."

She broke eye contact with the governor briefly, noticing there was another man in the living room, also dressed in a dark suit and tie. His face was somewhat familiar, but she couldn't place him. His gray hair was too long for a professional look, but only on the top of his head, making him look as if he wore a poorly fitted toupée. That haircut was memorable; she'd definitely seen him before.

"This is Wade Hebert, our attorney," Bachert said. "He will explain to you why I cannot allow you to interrogate my daughter. Tell me what you need to know, and I will ask her myself."

The attorney smiled and extended his hand, but Tess glared at him and his smile quickly withered. Then she turned her full attention to the governor.

"This is not an interrogation," Tess replied coldly. "Your daughter is not a suspect, she's a witness. Your attorney should've informed you by now that law enforcement has the right to interview minors without a parent—"

"Don't patronize me, Winnett!" Bachert snapped. He ran his hand angrily through his graying, buzz-cut hair. "All right, you can speak with her, but Wade and I will sit in."

She shook her head in disbelief. "But, sir, your daughter might not fully cooperate with you present. She might hold back."

"Are you insinuating my daughter's a liar? Or has something to hide? I can assure you she's done nothing illegal, nor has she any knowledge of wrongdoing."

"Your daughter is first and foremost a teenager, and girls her age keep secrets from their parents. Please consider the facts: we have a young girl missing, Kaylee Lewis, who's your daughter's best friend and a regular guest of your family. I'd assume you're as eager as we are to find out what happened to her and bring her home to her mother."

Bachert let out a sigh of frustration and shoved his hands in his pockets. "Of course, I want Kaylee to be found and brought back, what the hell are you insinuating?" He'd lowered the pitch of his voice to a menacing tone. "Are you planning to entrap my little girl into incriminating herself with respect to this sordid affair?"

"What sordid affair?" Tess reacted. "A kid's gone missing, she didn't come home last night, after visiting here. Your little girl's best friend," she added, angry with herself for raising her voice. If she was to win in that fight, she had to keep Bachert from getting under her skin. "What if Kaylee was your daughter? Wouldn't you want anything and everything done to ensure her safe return?"

"I understand all that, Agent Winnett, but I'm afraid I cannot allow you to speak with my daughter alone. End of story."

She let a threatening smile stretch the corners of her mouth. The governor might've been powerful, but she was holding a few trump cards too. "I'm sure your attorney can explain to you the concept and legal implications of obstruction of justice."

"There's no obstruction, if my client allows the interview in his presence," the lawyer quickly stated.

She didn't take her eyes off Bachert, but replied calmly, "It is, if it can be proven that his presence caused the witness to withhold essential facts and was duly forewarned."

The ensuing silence told Tess she'd struck a chord. Yet Bachert's eyes turned a steely shade of darker blue.

"Are you threatening me?" he said, leaning forward and lowering his voice to almost a whisper. He towered over Tess, making her feel the urge to take a step back.

She resisted, briefly wondering why she wasn't six-foot-three, to be on the same eye level with the officially elected bully.

"No, sir, I'm merely stating facts and procedure." She held her breath, waiting for his reaction. "Not to mention," she continued calmly, "if I call my boss and explain the situation, someone might overhear the call and find out that the highest elected official of this state doesn't care about missing children, even when he happens to know them personally."

"Damn you, Winnett!" he bellowed, inches away from her face, then turned and walked away with anger in his heavy steps.

She waited for a moment, giving him time to weigh his options. Damn *him* and the time he wasted... how come a parent couldn't see how precious every minute was when a child was missing?

"All right, you'll have your interview. Wade and I will listen in from the other room, but be careful with every word you say and every question you ask. I won't let you turn this situation into a political circus of any kind."

She nodded almost imperceptibly, then asked, "By the way, were you at home last night when Kaylee left?"

"No. By the time I came home, she was already gone. It was just Alice, her mother, and I at the dinner table."

"What time was that?"

"About six-thirty or so. Kaylee usually goes home before I get back. She has a dusk curfew, just like Alice."

"All right, then, I'm ready to sit with your daughter," Tess said, ready to follow his lead. "Let's not waste any more time."

"You'll do this in my home office," Bachert said, "but remember what I said. One wrong question, one twisted word, and I'll stop this interview on the spot."

"Understood," she replied reluctantly. The man wanted to have the last word no matter what.

"Winnett," he added, lowering his voice again to that menacing tone she'd heard before, "no one threatens me, you understand that? You'll have your way now, but I'll have your badge as soon as this is over."

She didn't flinch, didn't lower her eyes.

His eyebrows raised a little.

"Judging by your demeanor, you already know that," Bachert added, surprise poorly disguised in his voice. "And you don't care?"

She shook her head. "All I care about is finding that girl alive. The rest, you included, can go straight to hell."

6

INTERVIEW

Tess entered the large home office and gave it a critical look. It was cold and unwelcoming, and the massive desk covered in folders and stacks of neatly bound documents would've been intimidating to a young girl, even if she was familiar with it. Tess refused with a quick hand gesture the lawyer's invitation to take a seat behind the massive piece of oak furniture and had to refrain a smile, thinking of Governor Bachert's incredible cunning. By suggesting she sit at his desk, in his seat, while talking to his daughter, he wanted Alice to feel his presence looming in the room, a stern reminder to watch every word she was going to say to Tess.

He's smart, I'll give him that, Tess thought, looking around the room in search of a better option.

There was a large sofa by the window overlooking the park, and she opted to be seated there. Then a disapproving Wade Hebert left the room and, a moment later, Alice appeared in the doorway.

Tess expected an entitled, spoiled brat, raised in the image of her father, but Alice was nothing like that. She was rather shy and hesitant, visibly uncomfortable to be interviewed by Tess, but trying to be still and appear cool. She was failing by a long shot... She was nervous, tugging at the sleeves of her shirt and twisting strands of her brown hair.

She ventured a tiny smile, then asked, "Hi... where should I sit?"

Tess smiled and patted the sofa next to her. Seated there,

she would have her back at the office door that remained open.

The girl sat on the edge of the seat, turned slightly toward Tess, as if getting ready to run. Nervousness continued to make her fidget incessantly, and Tess allowed a few seconds of that to pass by, studying her movements carefully. She hadn't had the chance to ask Alice a single question yet, but the girl's entire body language reflected the demeanor of someone who was lying. Sometimes, that happened when people knew ahead of time that whatever the questions asked of them, they had every intention to lie. In other cases, specifically with shy or socially awkward people, that nervousness was nothing more than a sign of how stressful the situation was for them.

Too soon to tell.

"Hello, Alice," Tess finally said in the warmest and friendliest tone she could manage. "Thanks for agreeing to speak with me today."

The girl shrugged but didn't say anything.

"I know you're anxious to see Kaylee again safe and sound."

The girl's attention turned briefly toward the open office door with a quick flick of her head. "Yeah," she whispered. Her eyes avoided Tess's but stayed mobile and alert, as if she were following the erratic flight of an invisible insect.

"Walk me through everything that happened yesterday," Tess asked. "Let's start with school. What time did you see Kaylee in the morning?"

Alice folded her hands in her lap, but then started kneading her fingers together.

"Um, first period, I guess. That starts at eight."

"Then what happened?"

She groaned before replying, a quick reaction to what she must've thought was a stupid question. "School, what else?

Then we came here." She gave her kneaded fingers a quick break to grab a loose strand of hair and tuck it behind her ear.

"Was Kaylee with you at lunch?"

"Uh-huh." Her eyes now stared at Tess's shoes.

"What time was that?"

"Twelve," she replied quietly.

Tess had seen this in suspects and witnesses alike. When they couldn't distance themselves physically from the object of a lie, they sometimes distanced themselves through diminishing the length and intensity of their statements, as if stating the lie quickly and quietly would make it somehow fly under the investigator's radar.

"And then?" Tess continued, apparently having accepted the statement as true.

"Then more school," Alice mumbled. "You know what it's like," she ventured, making eye contact with Tess for a brief moment, then looking away.

"What time did you get here?"

Alice turned her head again to check the door, then lowered her voice. "About four."

"Was Kaylee with you?"

"Uh-huh." Her head swiveled again and then back with dizzying speed.

Who or what was she afraid of? Her parents had been away at work, there was no one to contradict her statements. *Oh, but there* was *someone,* Tess thought, remembering Deanne's statement about the Bachert household and the three full-time staff. *Okay, Miss Bachert, let's turn up the heat.*

"Can anyone corroborate your statement?" she asked quietly, hoping the watchdogs listening outside the office wouldn't choose that moment to barge in.

Alice frowned, seemingly confused. "What do you mean?"

"Like the house staff, for example," Tess replied calmly, not buying it for one moment that she didn't know the meaning of the word.

Alice pivoted her head toward the door again and quickly back, her long hair dancing around her shoulders. "Um, there was no one, really," she whispered. "We went straight to my room, so they couldn't have seen her, uh, I mean, us."

Tess smiled encouragingly. "House staff always know more than you give them credit for. It's their job." She watched as Alice started kneading her fingers again, shooting glances left and right of Tess like a desperate, cornered animal looking for a way out of a gaping trap. "How about we ask them?"

Alice swallowed hard, then reached out and grabbed Tess's hand with a trembling hand. "Please... don't ask them. I'll tell you, but please don't tell my dad."

Tess nodded. "I promise."

"Kaylee, um, wasn't here last night. She left after school, but I don't know where she went, 'cause she didn't tell me," Alice blurted.

Her body language still showed multiple signs of deception, but Tess didn't need that to know she was still lying. At 12:37 P.M., Kaylee's phone had pinged the cellular network in North Beach, not at school.

"Is this the first time you've covered for Kaylee with her mom?"

"Yes, I swear," Alice replied, a little louder, and meeting Tess's eyes for a prolonged moment.

Finally, a true statement, Tess thought.

"Alice, we know for sure when Kaylee left school. We tracked her phone. Let me give you one more chance to tell the truth.

When did she leave?"

Alice touched her forehead with her hand, as if to hide her eyes from the acute scrutiny, while color disappeared from her cheeks, leaving them a deathly pale.

"Right before lunch," she finally said.

"Where did she go?"

"To meet someone," Alice said, after checking the door one more time. "Her new boyfriend, I guess."

"Who is he, Alice?" It was Tess's turn to reach out and squeeze the girl's hand. "You understand how important this is, don't you?"

"She wouldn't say," Alice replied, her voice tearful and trembling. "She said it's her big secret. That one day she'd tell me, but not now."

Another nugget of truth, and Tess felt like cursing out loud. Not the truth she was searching for.

She squeezed Alice's hand again and said, "Kaylee could die if we can't find her now, immediately. This is serious."

The girl nodded, tears rolling down her cheeks.

"Think of anything that has changed in her life, something you might've heard her say, anything at all."

Alice sniffled and swallowed hard before speaking. "She's been really secretive lately," she whispered. "She's been sneaking out a lot, cutting classes when the teachers don't really pay attention, and I—I covered for her in school a few times. But never with her mom, I swear," she added, after briefly checking that door again.

Even if Bachert were standing right outside, he couldn't hear much of what was said. They kept their voices low; an obvious choice Alice had made that Tess was grateful for. Bachert must've been fuming.

"Has she changed in any other ways?" Tess asked. "Recently, I mean."

Alice tilted her head slightly, thinking. "Um, she's become almost mushy, all she talked about was him. How he makes her feel, how he talks to her, stuff like that. She's madly in love with that guy."

"Since when?"

"Oh, just a few days, but I don't think they went too far, you know. First base, maybe second?" Alice said, blushing a little.

"Do you know anything about this boyfriend? His name—"

She frowned and pulled back. "I already said she never told me his name."

"Oh, yes, you did, I apologize," Tess replied calmly. "How about his age? How old is he?"

The girl's eyes started chasing imaginary flies again. The time for truth had apparently passed.

"He's not old," she managed to say, fidgeting in her seat and giving her fingers another thorough work over. "He's young."

"How young?" Tess waited, but no sounds came out of Alice's mouth. "Alice, this is a matter of life and death. I know you want what's best for Kaylee, but you're not going to get her in any trouble, I promise."

"She said he's thirty-something," she whispered, then started sobbing quietly.

"Thirty-how-many is thirty-something?"

"She didn't say."

Tess clenched her jaws and ground her teeth but kept her apparent cool. "Did she tell you where she met him? She's a little young to be seeing a thirty-something man, isn't she?" Tess added, instantly regretful. Her question fueled Alice's sobs, and now the girl's shoulders heaved with every shattered breath.

"Now I'm in trouble with you," Alice whimpered, "and he's going to get in trouble with the cops, and Kaylee will never talk to me again. You people won't stop until you screw everyone's life. I should've shut up."

Tess touched the girl's shoulder, and Alice lifted her teary eyes to look at her. "Listen, if we find Kaylee alive and we bring her home safely, it will be because of you. You should be happy, knowing you helped us find her."

Alice nodded, sending waves into her long hair, but then pulled away from Tess. "Dad's lawyer said I can refuse to talk to you," she said, lifting her head and looking Tess straight in the eye, some of her father's fortitude coming across clearly. She'd raised her voice a little, just enough to be heard from outside the room.

"You lied to Kaylee's mom, and that's a serious matter," Tess replied, also her voice raised to be overheard from outside. At least she'd have some questions to answer to her father, if she wouldn't continue answering them for Tess. And maybe Bachert would find it wise to share.

Her moist eyes threw poisonous darts at Tess. "You promised," she said, her voice low and menacing, almost like her dad's.

As expected, the governor stepped quickly inside the room with his thousand-dollar-suit lawyer by his side. Tess stood and headed toward them.

"This interview is over," Bachert said. "Anything else, Agent Winnett, before you leave?"

"Yes, one more thing," she replied, then turned to face Alice, whose anger came across clearly in her scrunched features. "I know you love Kaylee, Alice, I have no doubt in my mind. Only a true, loving friend would give her such a beautiful rose. What was the occasion?"

Alice frowned, visibly confused. "What rose?"

7

SISTER

He'd been blessed to have been born into a wealthy and well-respected family, who loved him and nurtured him, leaving him wanting for nothing. Every dream fulfilled before he could even formulate it clearly in his mind. Every wish come true. Yes, he had to admit it, compared to others, he'd been truly blessed.

With one exception.

He had a twin sister.

And they'd always loved her more.

It even showed in the names the twins had been given at birth, to make everyone aware of how things really were in their family. The little runt's name was Aimée, French for beloved, while his name was David.

Plain, simple, David.

David, who?

Exactly.

How many Davids were there in this country? He'd recently had the curiosity to find out, but now he wished he hadn't. Turned out David was the third most popular name in the United States, with almost five million people labeled with it. Why even bother to give a child such a name?

Of course, back then, he didn't know that. He just resented how it sounded. Banal. Common. Meaningless. The driver's son was a David. Can you imagine? Being called the same as that idiot's Neanderthaloid offspring?

Back then, he'd resented how his mother's face lit up when

she called out his sister's name: Aimée, pronounced with impeccable French articulation, because she was, after all, French. She'd never given up being French, even after taking her husband's last name through marriage. She was now Dominique Bisset, their shared last name pronounced with the lingering "e" and a silent "t," precisely how the French would say it. In the presence of his wife, Alfred Bisset, an American born in Kentucky, swallowed the last consonant of his last name with flustered hesitation whenever he spoke his name.

While he was just David. His wasn't even a French name.

From the day he was born, she must have resented him and decided she loved her little girl far more. She must have said, during her endless labor, after giving birth to her daughter, that Aimée was enough; she'd only wanted one child, not two.

Yet he'd been born, nevertheless.

Dubbed David.

And reminded every day how meaningless he was in her eyes, especially by comparison with his perfect little sister.

In her mother's eyes, Aimée was a perfect, blue-eyed, blonde little angel with curly, long hair, and a voice like birdsong. Dominique loved to dress Aimée up, bought her new things every day, and never got bored combing through her long hair. As for David, she rushed getting him clothed, always a chore, always simply and almost rigidly, in slacks or shorts and a shirt, and almost always patted him on his back saying, "That's it, you're done, now go!" as if eager to get rid of him sooner.

Then she grabbed Aimée's hand and dragged her into her husband's office, and said cheerfully, "Look, Freddie, she looks just like me when I was her age!" And his dad would pick up the little bitch and fawn over her, completely forgetting he also had a son who watched quietly from the hallway.

By the time the twins turned five, David hated Aimée so much he could barely stand being seated next to her at the dinner table. But the worst was yet to come, in the form of a birthday cake he had to share with her that year. Even the birthday cake was hers first! The maid rolled it in on a serving cart, then set it on the table in front of them and lit the five animal-shaped candles.

He was filling up his lungs, getting ready to blow the candles out, with a secret and dark wish in mind, when Dominique intervened for her yet again.

"Wait your turn, David," she commanded. "She's just a little girl, don't be a bully. Your sister comes first."

Then she pushed the cake in front of beaming Aimée. She blew over the candles, but only extinguished two. Before she could replenish her lungs for another attempt, David pushed her aside and finished the job, the same dark and secret wish vivid, urgent, burning in his mind.

Aimée started crying.

His mother's hand landed loudly across his face with a searing slap that burned his eyes with unwanted tears.

He hadn't cried that night, although he'd been sent upstairs without being allowed to eat a slice of cake on his own birthday, all because of that stupid little bitch. He hadn't cried ever again.

Before he turned six, he'd seen the damage he could do with a little ingenuity. A discreet shove at exactly the right time had landed Aimée flat on her face, hitting the concrete hard after running around the pool. He'd rushed immediately to her side and fussed over her just like he'd seen Mother do, and then later, when Dominique arrived, he took a few steps back and soaked in every tear his mother cried over Aimée's broken ankle and scratched forehead.

His mother's pain was punishment for not loving him more. Aimée's pain was punishment for the runt's very existence.

It should've been worse. If there was any justice in the world, it should've been far worse.

The following year, Aimée fell down a flight of stairs and broke her shoulder. He took in his mother's pain like a man dying of thirst takes in water, eagerly, exhilarated with each drop of it. But Dominique's renewed attention for her little hurt angel fueled his rage even more.

If only she could love him too!

Maybe if he could show her that Aimée was not a little angel after all, she could turn and love him instead.

He'd planned it for months, wondering how to make it work. Then the perfect opportunity presented itself.

His parents were planning a ball and fundraiser at the house. His mother had fussed over what she and Aimée would wear for the occasion and had decided to order matching gowns for both of them in blue satin with rhinestone-encrusted hems.

The morning before the ball, when both gowns lay neatly on his mother's bed, he snuck in his parents' bedroom with a pair of gardening scissors and cut his mother's gown to shreds. He left Aimée's intact, because she was to be his scapegoat. He hid the shredded dress under Aimée's princess bed and put the scissors back in the gardener's shed.

Then he waited, like a hungry, yet patient, spider lurks in the shadows for its unsuspecting prey.

It was right after lunch when the maid rushed in and apologized for interrupting, then broke the news. Madame Bisset's gown was destroyed and was found under Aimée's bed. It seemed, by all appearances, that Aimée had taken the scissors to it.

His mother didn't even look at Aimée with a questioning look. "No," she stated calmly, "my little angel would never do that. It must've been David."

And she'd grounded him for a year, refusing to hear his sworn statements of innocence.

The following year, Aimée had a mishap in school, landing at the bottom of a flight of concrete steps with a broken leg, a twisted wrist, and a concussion. Unfortunately, not a broken neck.

Then, by the time the twins were preparing for their eleventh birthday, the stars aligned in the sky to make David's most secret wish come true.

They were splashing around in the pool with a couple of other kids from across the street, when Dominique had to go inside to take a phone call. The two visiting kids were splashing in the shallow end of the pool, paying no attention to him or Aimée, arguing bitterly over a blue foam pool noodle.

He dove quickly and pulled Aimée under the water, holding her firmly by her ankles until she stopped fighting. Her little body twitched two more times, then felt listless under the water, just as he was running out of air in his lungs.

He surfaced, giving Aimée another push down, toward the bottom of the pool, watching as her body sank slowly. He looked around carefully, watching for the tiniest sign of attention from the other two kids. Then, hearing his mother's voice approach, he started screaming.

"Mom! Help!" He dove to the bottom of the pool, and pretended he wanted to grab Aimée and lift her up, then came back for air, feigning out of breath, shattered gasps, then screamed some more, repeating his perfectly fabricated efforts.

Moments later, his father dove into the pool completely

clothed and resurfaced with Aimée's lifeless body in his arms. Forty minutes later, the EMS crew pronounced her dead at the scene.

The little runt was finally gone.

He had to hide behind closed doors, pretending he was devastated, to conceal the uncontrollable urge to grin that stretched his lips and the emotions that filled his chest with unspeakable ecstasy. His mother's wails fueled the state of exultation that had been with him the entire time, and the accounts of his bravery in attempting to save his sister massaged his yearning ego, albeit too little, too late.

He could be free, at last, to enjoy his mother's undivided love.

But that still wasn't there for him to enjoy, as if an unspoken curse lay on top of his head making him unlovable by the only woman who mattered in his life.

Brokenhearted and almost insane with grief, Dominique had shut everyone out, including her husband and son. Alone and wandering aimlessly through the enormous house, the man and his young boy barely spoke to each other, both pining for Dominique's attention.

And yet, whenever he found himself alone behind closed doors, David smiled widely, feeling a sense of excitement like never before. He relived the death of his sister over and over again in his mind, obsessing about every detail, recalling every thrashing of her agonizing body against his firm grip, forever burned into his memory.

A few days later, the family had announced the funeral and where it was going to take place. That day, eager to relive his most treasured memory, he walked to the nearby mortuary, snuck inside, found the room where the dead bodies were kept, and hid in a broom closet.

From there, he could see, through the keyhole, how the mortician let out Aimée's blood and replaced it with a clear, smelly fluid. The mortician fussed over her naked body for a long time, but David couldn't see everything that was going on; even more reason for his imagination to run wild.

Later, after everyone went home, he searched for his sister's body in the deserted mortuary and found it displayed in an open mahogany casket, at the center of a solemnly decorated room with hundreds of roses in bloom, ready for the memorial service scheduled for the next morning.

He approached Aimée's body, afraid to breathe, to make even the tiniest sound. She'd been dressed in one of her favorite dresses and wore her favorite shoes. She seemed almost alive, her skin rosy and her lips red, no trace left of the bluish skin and pale lips he so well remembered from the side of the pool. He touched her cheeks and she didn't wake up. Her face was cold, and his fingers felt a powdery substance that he quickly recognized as makeup. It smelled somewhat like his mother's cosmetics that he sometimes snuck into his bedroom to savor, the familiar scent bringing the woman he missed closer to him somehow.

Aimée's body was surrounded with roses in bloom, and a single, long-stemmed pink rose was placed on her chest, fresh, pristine petals touching the girl's lips. Surrounding the casket, dozens of roses were fanned out, as if she laid at the center of a single, open bloom, the casket barely visible underneath blossoms, leaves, and stems.

His hand moved from Aimée's face to her body and he squeezed. She was soft, just as he remembered her in the pool. She felt cold though, but that didn't stop him. What he felt was entirely new to him, an urgency like never before, lighting an unspeakable fire in his groin, driving him to do things he never thought he would, to find his first release.

Later, in the safety of his bedroom, and after having spent hours reliving his experience in a cleansing shower, his only regret was that she hadn't been alive, to scream and fight him off, but still be overpowered.

Taken.

Bearing his mark forever.

8

COFFEE FOR TWO

By the time she got to the car, her phone rang, displaying Donovan's name. She hoped he might've somehow worked a miracle with his technology, because she'd failed to extract anything useful from Alice Bachert, and had done little more than waste precious time. The twenty-four hour marker was approaching quickly, and with every passing minute, the chances of finding Kaylee alive plummeted.

She unlocked her SUV and quickly started the engine to restore the flow of cold air and make the vehicle usable again, while taking Donovan's call.

"What do you have?" she asked, knowing he'd never call without new information.

"A possible lead," he replied. "I tracked both phones, Alice's and Kaylee's, going back two weeks. For the most part, the girls spent their time at school, or at the Bachert residence, rarely at Kaylee's. But there was one other place that showed up on the map a lot, a coffee shop called Café Dream. It's on—"

"I know where that is, D," she said, shifting into gear and peeling off. "You're amazing, you know that?"

"I know it, and I'm glad you know it too, Winnett," he quipped. "It took you a while to figure it out, huh?"

She laughed. "Going to Café Dream now." She almost hung up but then decided to share the dismal results of her sit-down with Alice. "I don't have any info on our unsub yet, other than he's thirty-something and he might've given Kaylee a rose. He also seems new in her life; someone she might've only recently met. Our unsub remains an unknown subject for now."

"I don't think you've ever come out of an interview so empty-handed."

"Tell me something I don't know," she mumbled. "That girl didn't let more than three truthful words come out of her mouth. Let's see what the café can do for us. I'm there," she added, right before ending the call, tapping the red button on the steering wheel.

The café was bustling with customers, the chatter loud and happy, a guaranteed result of the combined effects of caffeine and sugar. The blend of smells in the café was intoxicating, alluring, hints of caramel and cinnamon mixed with the stronger scent of dark roast java.

Almost all the tables were taken, and there was a line at the order counter. Most of the seated customers were young people, some working on their laptops, but a few teenagers too, all visibly well-off. Teenagers who could afford to spend five, maybe even ten dollars on a cup of coffee, while doing a dress rehearsal for their soon-to-come days of clubbing and barhopping.

Three baristas went through rushed movements like automatons, probably doing their jobs without paying much attention to their surroundings. They processed orders and filled them incredibly fast and yet, every few seconds, one of them managed to wipe the counter or rush to clean a recently vacated table.

She flashed her badge above the counter and immediately got one of the barista's attention, a thin, almost gaunt Asian girl who couldn't've been a day older than seventeen. Her green name tag read "Lin."

"What can I get you?" she asked, ready to input an order.

Her apparent cutting into the line earned her angry glares from the waiting customers.

"Not here for coffee," she clarified. "I need you and your colleagues to look at some photos and tell me if you've seen these people before."

Two of the five people waiting in line decided they didn't need coffee all that badly and vanished without a word. They must've had some issue with the law, possibly as meaningless as an unpaid parking ticket or as serious as an outstanding arrest warrant.

Tess decided to use that to her advantage and hung her badge in plain sight, on her jacket pocket. Surprisingly for that rush hour, no other customers lined up after her.

Lin signaled her two colleagues. One was a young, freckled man who made the drinks, paying attention to every detail and hunching over each order, toiling until it was perfect, yet managing to do all that incredibly fast, whether cappuccinos, lattes, or espressos. The other barista, a pleasant-looking brunette, was taking orders at the drive-through window.

After taking the last order and putting it into the system, Lin circled the counter and joined Tess.

"Tell me, what do you need?" Lin asked in a pleasant, soft voice.

Tess displayed Kaylee's photo on her phone. "Have you seen this girl before?"

"Oh, yes," she replied, nodding enthusiastically and grinning widely. "She's a regular and comes with a friend, another girl."

Tess flipped to Alice's photo, and showed it to Lin.

"Yes, that's the girl," she replied just as enthusiastically.

"Did you notice anyone else with these girls?"

"Um, let me think," she said, then pointed at an empty table toward the window. "That's where they usually sit. Yes, I think I've seen them with a man or maybe two, at different times, not sure." She turned toward the counter and beckoned her colleague. "Hey, Ramon, get over here," she called, her voice now surprisingly strong.

The young man leaned over the counter to look at the photos.

"Yeah, I've seen these two chicks. They come here a lot. The blonde goes for caramel cappuccinos, and the other gal drinks black Americana."

Tess smiled. "Good memory, but that's not what I need. Have you seen them with anyone else?"

"Some men, for sure," Ramon replied. "I remember because Jeanie and this one were talking crap about one of the men," he added, pointing at Lin, who promptly elbowed his ribs. "Why? What happened? I haven't seen them in here today, but it's still early."

"Have you seen this girl leaving by herself with one of the men?" Tess asked, showing him Kaylee's photo again.

"Couldn't tell you, but I'm sure Jeanie could, if she'll let you look at the tapes. She's the manager, you know."

Tess looked at the ceiling and saw a couple of tiny cameras, cleverly disguised in the décor.

Ramon went over to Jeanie, whispered something in her ear, then took over for her, while the woman wiped her hands on her apron and came to talk with Tess.

"I hear you need to look at the surveillance tapes," she said coldly. "What's this about? We're not allowed to show them to anyone without a warrant."

"A girl's missing and we're trying to find her," Tess replied, hiding an eyeroll. "I'd rather we save time than waste it with issuing warrants."

"Let me see," she said, looking at the Kaylee's photo. "Oh, I know her, yeah, she's the one with that guy," she added, looking at Lin with a meaningful glance. "*Him*, you remember?"

"Yeah, I remember," Lin replied. "I know the guy you're talking about, but are you sure he was with her?"

"Positive," Jeanie replied. "I remember thinking to myself that you'd have to be as beautiful as she is to score a date like that."

"When was that?" Tess asked.

"Um, more than once, that's for sure," Jeanie replied. "Last time I saw them together was two days ago."

"Did they leave together?"

She propped her hands on her hips, staring thoughtfully at the floor for a brief moment as if trying to decide what to do, then turned to Tess. "Come, follow me. I'll show you the tapes."

She led the way into a room barely the size of a closet, where they kept supplies in large cans. On a small table, a dusty keyboard and two monochrome screens were connected to an antiquated, low-resolution surveillance system.

"Thanks," Tess said, getting ready to call Donovan for assistance.

"Allow me," Jeanie offered. "I'll rewind to the place where I saw them together."

The tape whirred while the screen rushed through images shown almost too quickly to make anything out of them, but the barista knew exactly what she was looking for.

"There, this is one of the guys," she said, and let the video run for a while.

The time stamp showed 3:42 P.M., six days ago, and the

man who had approached the table where the two girls sat had greeted them and took a seat with them for a few minutes, but then left by himself. Judging by the body language, barely distinguishable in the grainy, black-and-white video, the conversation had been banal, neither party showing much interest in the other, although it was obvious they knew each other well.

Tess took a screenshot of the video and sent it to Donovan with a quick note.

The whirring resumed, and the tape stopped again, this time showing a different man.

"And this is the guy Lin and I were talking about," Jeanie said.

"What do you remember about him?" Tess asked, focusing on her instead of the video.

"He was... stunning," the young woman admitted, the statement bringing some fire to her cheeks. "I rarely think of men like that, but this one... I remember envying that girl, and I wished that was me, sitting with him at that table."

"Have you seen him in here before?"

"No. I would've remembered. He came in a few times these past few days, only when these two girls were here, but he only cared about the blonde."

"How could you tell?" Tess asked.

"You'll see," Jeanie replied. She let the video run for a few minutes, at times playing it on fast until Tess stopped her.

The man had entered the café and approached the girls' table directly, without buying a cup of coffee. Kaylee had responded to his arrival in a visible way, smiling widely and tilting her head in a flirtatious gesture. They shook hands and talked, while Alice sat there, silent, ignored. After a while, probably tired of being the third wheel, Alice stood and left, barely getting a goodbye wave from Kaylee. Then the two remained at the table, heads close together, holding hands, talking, for exactly forty-two minutes. Then they left together, the man politely holding the door for her and briefly touching her back while she walked past.

In total, forty-nine minutes of video recording of what seemed to be her strongest lead yet. And not for one moment had that man turned his head or shown his face to the camera. He had not bought anything from the café, so there was no record of any transactions, and he'd walked away with Kaylee two days ago.

But Kaylee went missing yesterday. What had happened two days ago? Where did they part ways? Where else did they go together?

"How about other videos? Older recordings?" Tess asked, feeling a wave of frustration threatening to turn into a slew of oaths.

"We override the tapes every seven days," Jeanie replied.

"Can you give me a detailed description, maybe sit with a sketch artist?"

She shifted her weight from one foot to the other, seemingly uncomfortable at the thought.

"Really, what happened?" Jeanie asked. "Has he done something to that girl?"

Witnesses and their morbid curiosity, Tess thought, thankful she'd seen the tapes without having to make any threats.

"We don't know that," Tess replied. "We just need to find this man and ask him a few questions, that's all."

"Right," Jeanie mumbled, while the tape whirred again. "You know, I'm not an idiot. Did he kill her? If the feds are involved, she's dead, isn't she?"

Tess hesitated, reluctant to share any case details with a civilian, especially a witness. Witness testimony can be corrupted by many things: lack of perception and focus, faulty attention to detail, the passing of time. She didn't want to add to the list by giving Jeanie any information.

But she needed an ally.

"No, as far as we know, Kaylee's only missing. We need to speak to anyone who might've seen her or know where she might be, and this is urgent."

"There," Jeanie said, and the whirring stopped. On the grainy screen, she saw the man's face, barely distinguishable, but his face, nevertheless. The video had been taken five days ago, when he'd entered the café looking up, straight into the camera for a brief moment, most likely unaware a camera was there, or maybe not concerned at all. Then he had joined Kaylee at their usual table by the window.

She had his face.

It was something Donovan could work with.

It was eerily familiar.

9

COLD

The first feeling she realized was how cold she was.

It wasn't just the air being chilly; it was as if the cold had entered her bones and had coiled inside them like a living creature, nesting, multiplying, growing, invading her body.

Kaylee tried to move, and this time she felt her arm pull against a restraint wrapped around her wrist. A weak wave of excitement coursed through her veins, realizing that she'd been able to move her arm, even if a tiny bit. She tried again, this time harder, and felt her right arm twist in its restraint, her fingers touching her thigh.

She tried to flex her leg but couldn't, something tugging at her ankle was keeping her from doing more than just bend her knee a little. It was a start… whatever it was he'd given her was wearing off, and she could feel and move again.

She lifted her head off the pillow, feeling dizzy and nauseated, and looked around. She almost fainted at the sight of blood leaving her body, drop by drop. The porcelain bowl was almost full, but the drip was coming out of her vein slowly, one or two seconds passing between two drops. The needle in her arm was hooked to a transparent piece of tubing that passed through a device meant to control the flow with a screw pressing the tubing between two small metallic plates. Her wrist was tied to the bench with a soft, faux fur cuff in dark red, almost the color of her blood.

Roses were laid all around her naked body, hundreds of them, a sickening oval of perfectly pink blooms, their fresh scent evocative of turned earth after rain or a freshly dug grave in the fall.

Then she saw him.

Only a few feet away, partially hidden behind a huge canvas set up on a low easel, he worked furiously, the sound of his brush scraping against the canvas unmistakable, the scent of fresh oil paint filling the studio. She could hear him squeezing paint tubes, rattling objects on the small table by his side. Every few minutes, he approached to study her face or arrange a strand of her hair, then rushed back to work some more.

The sun filled the studio again, making it more bearable than the darkness she'd endured for endless hours. Soon there would be some warmth too, she hoped. And maybe, just maybe, once he finished his painting, he'd let her go.

She started sobbing quietly, sadness and despair ripping through her chest and shattering her breath. She thought she'd found true love in the romantic, charming, and breathtakingly handsome man she'd met in the café. She'd enjoyed their long talks, walking hand in hand with the man of her dreams, while almost all women they encountered shot her glances filled with envy. She'd felt loved, admired, wanted. Overnight, the schoolgirl had grown up to become a woman in love. She'd yearned for his touch, for his kisses, for all the love he was willing to give. She'd been dreaming of the first night when she'd be alone with him, ready to submit to his every desire, needing to, with every fiber in her being.

But not like that... Not bound to a bench, trembling and freezing while blood left her body, while she was slowly dying. The man she'd fallen in love with was a monster. What was going to happen to her?

"No, no, no, no!" he shouted, rushing toward her angrily

with heavy footfalls marking his words in a sickening rhythm. He yanked a tissue from a box and tapped her cheeks dry with careful moves. "You're ruining your makeup. I'm not finished with your face yet!"

He held his index finger in the air close to her face in an unspoken warning. His face was transformed, no longer warm and charming. The charismatic, blue-gray eyes she'd fallen in love with were now cold, filled with resentment and hate.

Terrified beyond words, she watched as he turned the screw on the device attached to the transparent tubing, releasing the flow of blood drops faster.

She whimpered, unable to stop the flow of bitter tears. This time, she heard her own voice clearly.

"Why?" she asked, her voice loaded with immense sadness.

"Stop crying already," he said, pulling out another tissue and drying her tears. "You were always a spoiled brat. Now look what you've done." He picked up the makeup brush and started adjusting her eyeshadow.

"I love you, David," she whispered, her words accompanied by fresh tears.

"Hush, now," he said, continuing to work on her face. He added a few drops of fresh blood to the eye shadow scraped from the makeup kit and mixed them together into a crimson-hued paste. Then he started applying it gently on her swollen eyelids. "Be still, and when I'm done, I promise you'll get what you most secretly want." A lustful smile tugged at the corner of his lips.

"Why did you do this to me?"

"What, my dear?" he asked casually, touching up her lipstick, unperturbed, absentminded.

"Drug me, tie me up…" She let a long, tear-filled sigh escape her lips. "I would've done anything for you."

He looked at her critically, then picked up a small hairbrush and arranged a few locks of her hair.

"You're doing it already," he replied, looking at her with a trace of the admiration she'd seen in his eyes before, when she was falling in love with him. "We're achieving great things together, you and I. You will be remembered forever, your perfection intact, your beauty admired by the whole world. Just wait until you see your portrait. I'm almost ready."

His words were not soothing her fears. There was an unspoken omen in his voice, a promise of despair, of more anguish, of unspeakable darkness yet to come.

"But stop crying. I already have to compensate for the swelling in your face, and that's not easy, you know. You'll get what you want, I promise."

"What?" she managed to ask, holding her breath, terrified to imagine what that must've been in his twisted mind.

"You, me," he whispered, caressing her freezing skin with cold fingers, gently, probably careful not to smudge her makeup. "Our love, fulfilled like none other in the history of man's incessant search for passion."

"No…" she whimpered, struggling to set herself free of her restraints. "Please… let me go. I'm cold, and I'm scared. I want to go home."

"It's always about you and what you want, isn't it, princess?" The anger had returned in his voice, and his eyes threw hateful darts.

She tried to focus and think. Maybe she could make him let her go after finishing the painting. But could she really believe that?

"No, David," she whispered, swallowing her tears, "it's about you. I want to make you happy. I'll do whatever you want me to."

He thrust his chin out and clenched his jaw. She could see knotted muscles dance underneath the skin as his entire body tensed. A lopsided smirk stretched his lips.

"We'll see about that," he said in a menacing tone. "We're perfect beings, and there are only two such perfect beings in the entire world, Aimée, you and I. Once we become one, we'll be memorable, and the memory of you will live forever above my mantle."

He didn't even remember her name! Kaylee's thoughts raced, desperately looking for a way out. But there was no reasoning with him... Seemed that the more she tried, the worse it got. All she could hope for was that someone would find her before it was too late, before the last drop of blood had left her body.

She wanted to scream, as loudly as she could, in an irrational hope that someone would hear her. That her mother would hear her.

"Don't drug me again, please," she asked instead. "I want to see everything you want to do to me," she added, fear gripping her throat as she uttered the words. "I want to share it with you. Please don't drug me."

He smiled widely. This time the smile had some of the old warmth she remembered well.

"I wouldn't dream of it, my dear." He tilted his head as if to look at her face from a different angle. "When I take you, every fiber in your body will be screaming my name. And then, there will be only me."

10

AGAIN

Tess slammed the SUV door and started the engine, then took off, leaving the parking lot with tires screaming against the asphalt.

"That girl doesn't even know how *not* to lie," she mumbled, backtracking her earlier drive toward the governor's house. "Like father, like daughter. What is it with these people? Do they take truth-suppression pills or something?" She ended her rant with a couple of oaths, then focused.

Alice.

Her again.

She held all the answers but was just as willing to share them as a weathered Freemason with nothing left to lose.

"Oh, but she *does* have something to lose," Tess mumbled again. "Let's see what dear old dad has to say when I bust his little girl for making false statements."

She checked the time just as she was pulling over in front of the Bachert residence. It was almost noon. The twenty-four hours were almost up, and she was still chasing lies, while Kaylee was fighting for her life somewhere. Maybe. If she was still alive.

She banged on the door angrily, and the governor opened the door, visibly surprised. He must've been ready to leave, being that he was carrying a briefcase in his hand.

"Agent Winnett, what now?"

His broad shoulders blocked her entry.

"I need to speak with Alice immediately," she said, her eyes firmly locked with his.

"I'm sorry, Agent Winnett, but my daughter no longer wishes to answer your questions. Now if you'll excuse—"

"What, we're going to do this all over again? I can question her now, in your presence or not, or I can have her arrested for making false statements to a federal agent. Your call."

Without another word, he stepped out of the doorframe, letting her in. Based on his reaction, he already knew Alice had lied to her and had been advised on how to cooperate.

Once inside, Bachert closed the door, and Wade Hebert, the Bacherts' lawyer, rushed to meet her.

"Agent Winnett," he said, "you do realize, I hope, that a minor cannot be held accountable for any statement she might've made, even alleging she has made such a misleading statement intentionally. An underage person cannot fully comprehend the weight of such a statement, not to mention distinguish clearly along the fine lines between right and wrong. We can argue it was made in error—"

"Ah, save it," Tess said, turning toward Bachert. "Where is she?"

A few moments later, Bachert brought his daughter into his home office. Judging by the firm grip he had on the girl's arm, she was participating against her will. She'd been crying, her swollen, red eyes a testimony to that, but the glances she threw Tess were fierce, not subdued.

"The time you wasted could've cost Kaylee her life," Tess said, skipping past the niceties and going for the blood. "If that proves to be true, I will see that you are charged and held accountable for it, to the full extent of the law."

Color drained from the girl's face, and she sat on a nearby chair, in front of her father's massive desk. Hebert wanted to intervene, but Bachert stopped him with a hand gesture.

"Who is this man, Alice?" Tess asked, putting the security feed screenshot in front of her.

"I don't know," she replied, fidgeting in place, her voice a higher pitch than normal. "How would I know? You can barely see anything—"

"Because that's you, at the table with him and Kaylee, and that was two days ago. How many men have you been having coffee with at Café Dream two days ago?"

Bachert was fuming, staring at his daughter in anger and disbelief, but thankfully, he didn't intervene.

Alice started sobbing hard, burying her face in her hands. "I don't know, all right? It could've been the PE teacher, or Kaylee's old boyfriend. Or this other guy."

"You're busy, aren't you, missy," the governor mumbled, but Tess pleaded silence with a quick, imperative glance and he stopped talking.

"What other guy?"

She shrugged, still sobbing. "Just some guy. He talked to us, and that was it."

"No, that wasn't it, Alice," Tess replied, showing Alice a later image of her leaving the café. "No, he talked with Kaylee until you got bored and left. Remember him now?"

"He could've been the PE teacher, I just can't—"

"Alice!" Bachert bellowed, causing his daughter to startle.

"I don't know his name," she replied quietly, subdued. "I already told you that, but you won't believe me."

"He didn't introduce himself when he sat at the table?"

"No," she whimpered, wiping her face with the back of her hand. "He already knew Kaylee and completely ignored me."

Damn, Tess thought, her mind racing through various

scenarios. Who could that man have been, and how could she get to the truth? Was that man a casual acquaintance? Or the predator, setting his sights on his prey? Donovan was already cleaning up the grainy videos, and Kaylee's mother would have a look at those photos, but Tess didn't hold her breath for any of that yielding results.

"What did he talk about?" she asked.

"Um, nothing," Alice replied. "He just kept staring at Kaylee and telling her how incredibly beautiful she was."

"And that didn't seem strange to you, a thirty-something man just sitting at your table and complimenting your best friend?"

Alice raised her head and looked at Tess with a clear expression in her eyes. She must've thought Tess was an idiot. "Have you seen Kaylee's photo?" she asked, her voice tinged with disbelief. "Have you even seen it, really? She's amazing! She could model for anyone she chooses; she could star in movies; she could do any of that. Of course, her mother won't let her," she spat the words, "but Kaylee was planning to do it anyway."

Finally, something interesting, a thin, wispy lead, so fragile it could shatter in the blink of an eye. Worth pursuing, nevertheless.

"Is it possible this man was Kaylee's secret boyfriend?" Tess asked, forcing her tone to become friendlier, less frantic.

Alice thought about it for a moment, to Tess's experienced eye, it was obvious she was weighing in whether to admit it or not.

"Y—yes, I believe it could be him," Alice reluctantly admitted.

"Why is that?" Tess asked.

"Since the day she met him, she's been different, I told you that already," Alice replied, visibly irritated with Tess. "If I have to tell you the same things three times, we'll never be done here, and you'll never find Kaylee," she added, with a scornful grin on her face.

It took all of Tess's self-control to not slap her across the face.

"And you'll tell it to me again, until I'm satisfied you're telling the truth, assuming you even know what that is," she replied instead. "When did Kaylee first meet this man?"

Alice groaned. "At the café, about two weeks ago."

"How often do you girls go to that café, anyway?" Tess asked, and she could've sworn she saw a glimmer of gratitude on Bachert's stern face.

"Um, every day, almost," she replied quickly and quietly, lowering her head and hiding her eyes behind the curtain of long, silky hair. "If the weather is good."

"And how many times has this man joined you?"

"I can't remember," Alice replied. "I didn't pay any attention."

"If we have to spend countless hours going through weeks of videotapes—"

"This is your last warning," Bachert interrupted. To Tess's amazement, he was talking to his daughter, not to her.

"Four or five times," Alice admitted. "But I don't know what happened, because I usually left early. They didn't want me there. She was so happy to see him, whenever he showed up, she melted. Gross."

Somewhere, in those two weeks since she'd met that man, Kaylee had become a different person. Was she lured by someone who knew exactly how to press her buttons?

Kaylee's disappearance frustrated Tess immensely, and

now she understood why. It wasn't just time running out fast, and, with every vanishing second, Kaylee's chances of survival ebbing away like the unstoppable tides. It wasn't even how powerless that made her feel. No, it was something else. There were no prior victims to be autopsied, forensics to be analyzed, family members to be interviewed, a signature to be discovered, or an MO. She couldn't deliver the profile of the abductor, because there were no victims, no insight into his methods, his preferences, a trace of what his personality was like. Of whom he was. Of how he preyed.

The only profile she could deliver was Kaylee's. If she could completely understand who the girl was and what made her tick, she could begin to understand who her captor was and why he had chosen her.

Tess closed her eyes briefly and put her hand up, asking for a moment to think. Who was Kaylee?

A girl who made her own bed, concerned with how her best friend would react if her room was messy. Or was that bed made for him, the mysterious man she maybe hoped would come to her house? A beautiful girl who knew the value of her looks and wanted to model, to act. To be seen. Admired. Adulated.

Loved.

A girl who visited the governor's house on a daily basis and saw how the upper echelon lived. Everything neat and carefully arranged, vases filled with fresh flowers, peaceful beauty in all surroundings. Kaylee wanted that for herself. Her neat room, the rose in the crystal vase, the art magazines... all that was her way to bring that kind of life into hers, even if just tiny bits of it. She'd seen it, she'd craved it, she was weaving dreams of it with shards of reality sewn into their fabric.

Why the art magazines, though?

She opened her eyes and looked around. No signs of high-value art. Just the typical furniture store paintings. The Bacherts' investments might've been into something else.

"Are you into art at all?" Tess asked Alice, but then looked at the governor too. He frowned.

"No," Alice replied, "but Kaylee was, out of the blue. I hated that boring crap."

"Tell me more," Tess asked excitedly.

"We were normal kids," Alice replied. "You know, MTV, music, dance clubs," she whispered in a low voice, hoping her father wouldn't hear her.

"Jeez, Alice," he mumbled angrily.

"We didn't really go, Dad," she replied in a whimpering voice. "You always think what's worst of me. We just watched it on TV."

Damn Bachert again, intervening at all the wrong times. "Tell me about the art," Tess insisted.

"Art's for old people," she said dismissively. "But lately Kaylee wanted to visit museums instead of going to the café or hanging out at the mall."

"Since when?"

"I don't know." She gave it more thought under Tess's uncompromising scrutiny. "Since the past couple of weeks or so. I hoped she'd get over it, but no. She was obsessed with the stupid art and pining over that guy."

"Wait here," Tess said, springing to her feet. "I'll be back in a few minutes."

She rushed out the door and then to her car. Soon, she was standing impatiently in front of a street corner newspaper stand.

"Show me all the art magazines you have," she demanded. A few moments later, she left with a small pile of magazines, some of which she had seen in Kaylee's bedroom.

Back at the Bacherts, she sat in front of Alice and pushed a copy of *Art Review* on the desk in front of her.

"I want you to go through this magazine carefully and tell me if you recognize anyone. Or anything."

Alice stared at the magazine but didn't touch it. Frustrated and desperate for time, Tess flipped through the first few pages of the magazine angrily, almost tearing the pages.

"Look, damn it, just look and tell me if you recognize anyone."

"Close it," Alice said quietly, as if afraid to touch the glossy paper. She'd turned pale, as if she'd seen a ghost.

"Why? You won't even look through it?" Tess asked, bewildered.

"No," Alice replied, just as quietly. "The man you're looking for is on the front cover."

11

ARTIST

David had gone through adolescence as the frustrated, rejected son of Dominique Bisset, whose heart had never healed after the loss of her young daughter. Day after day, for years, she refused to leave her room, withering under the burden of the loss she'd suffered.

Fresh roses were brought to her room every day, her only interest into anything of this world. Her son and her husband, both shunned away vigorously, and, after a while, probably forgotten, resigned to keep each other silent company in everlasting, all-encompassing gloom.

His mother would never love him; David had to admit, after a few years had passed since Aimée's death. Nothing had changed in the way his mother felt about her only son.

Memories of that day at the pool still stirred something inside him, but too much time had passed for the feelings and the memories to be fresh, intact, and satisfying as he wanted them to be. Instead, the fog of time had fallen thick, leaving him yearning for something that no warm body could ever provide.

There was no girlfriend in young David's life, even well into his teenage years, nor was there any interest for the opposite sex, or the same sex, for that matter. When he turned sixteen and vehemently refused to have a birthday party, his father grew worried about the boy's total lack of socializing with other kids his age and decided it was time to do something.

Alfred's acumen included shrewd, multimillion-dollar

business transactions in the field of steel and metal fabrication, at the expense of his empathic side. A hardened businessman, Alfred had no insight into how to give his son a normal life or motivate him into becoming a teenager he could engage with. He never thought of taking fishing or camping trips with the boy; David would've loved the opportunity to spend any amount of undivided time with a parent. Instead, he consulted numerous psychologists, sparing no expense for the well-being of his son and permanently grief-stricken wife. Eventually, he took the advice of the one shrink who recommended he use the opportunity to kindle his wife's maternal instincts and took his concerns about David to her.

Dominique had listened to Alfred's account of David's social disinterest with an absentminded gaze into emptiness. Then she stood, tightened her robe's sash around her gaunt body, and said, "If that's what's expected of me, fine, I'll do it."

Starting the following day but going through the motions unenthusiastically, she started getting involved in David's life. Unfortunately for both of them, she wasn't ready to give the yearning child the love he was missing; instead, all she could bring herself to do was ask her son about school and friends, in a long list of daily questions that reminded David of interrogations seen in some old war movies.

She wasn't harsh; no, she tried to be gentle. But she forgot his answers the moment he spoke them, then asked him the same questions again moments later. She encouraged David to have friends over and introduce them to her, and soon thereafter forgot their names. One hour later, she forgot completely she had guests at the house, and acted surprised when she ran into them by the pool.

After having yearned for his mother's attention for years,

David grew sick of it. That wasn't love; it was a chore, probably imposed by his moronic and permanently absent father to ease his own guilt about having a failing son. His mother's questions weren't the attention he was looking for. It was a form of inquisition, mixed with further proof she didn't care about him at all, and she never would.

He'd never had a mother; that was the sad truth. Aimée had had a mother, but he never did. As for his father, he had no use for the ever-absent and meddling idiot who held his money hostage.

The death of his paternal grandfather a few years back had left him with a sizeable trust that he couldn't access until age twenty-five or the death of both parents.

Whichever came first.

But he had to wait. If his parents were to die before he turned eighteen, the balding family attorney with chronic halitosis would grab the reins of his life and probably drive him mad. Not worth risking it.

Days flew by, now that he had a plan. He graduated from high school with impressive results and had been accepted to both Princeton and Yale. He chose a business major at Princeton and was off to school a couple of months before he came of age.

Eighteen.

The magical number carried a strong bouquet of freedom on pristine rose petals in his daydreams. In his nightmares too. What if he'd get caught? How could he kill his parents without anyone suspecting?

More important, would the sight of his mother's body being laid to rest, blood dripping from her vein, have the same effect he remembered with lustful yearnings from his secret past?

What would he do then?

Just a few months later, around Christmas, when he was home visiting, the perfect opportunity presented itself. His parents were invited to attend a family wedding in Dallas. He refused to participate, but eagerly counted the days until their departure.

The night before their scheduled flight on the family-owned jet, he snuck onto the tarmac and nicked the plane's hydraulic lines. He then carefully wrapped the lines in rags, to slow the fluid leak and prevent warning lights from coming on before takeoff. He also didn't want to risk having a puddle get the seasoned pilot's attention. He even tied the rags in place with a few pieces of twine, knowing that once the plane had taken off, the pressure inside the fluid lines would accelerate the leak. But he wanted that plane to reach cruising altitude before the pilot would notice something was wrong; as such, he'd be unable to do anything. Without hydraulic fluid under pressure, his commands would not be transmitted to the plane's controls. It would crash, ideally where no one would find the bodies.

The plane went down somewhere over the Gulf of Mexico, just as he'd planned. Witnesses soaking in the sun on a yacht nearby stated the plane had burst into flames midflight.

A few weeks later, the investigation had been officially closed, and probate was completed.

David Bisset was free. And rich beyond his wildest dreams.

His only regret was that his parents' funeral was an empty-casket, symbolic event, robbing him of the opportunity to see his mother laid on a cold slab, her body surrounded by roses, like his most cherished of memories. But he'd traded that opportunity for the perfect crime and had gotten away with it.

He didn't waste any time after his parents' death. Completely disinterested in his father's business, he entrusted that to the board members with the only request that they make him lots of money each year. Then he went back to college to study business, a major for which he had zero interest.

For many months, he did exactly what was expected of him, even if the man who'd had any expectations out of David was gone. He studied, he tried to make friends, he even got himself a girlfriend, a shy and slightly nerdy heir of a technology company from Silicon Valley by the name of Nicole. Her French-sounding name got his interest more than her thin waist and undulating hips.

Yearning to be admired by everyone around him, and somehow failing to see his wits and his wealth did very well from that perspective, in addition to his physical beauty, he took modeling engagements for high-paying manufacturers of fashion apparel and cosmetics, like Gucci and Dolce & Gabbana, adding fame to everything else he had going. From the outside, he was the epitome of success.

Yet all that time, he struggled with daydreams and nightmares, both equally disturbing, both leaving him in a state of sexual arousal from which there was no release. Nicole was there and eager to please, but his erections withered the moment he touched her warm body. His mind was filled with unclear plans to change something in his life, only he didn't know what. The memory he tried so desperately to conjure during his intimate times was almost completely gone, leaving him devoid and desperately craving release.

Until one day, after his last class, when he took a detour through one of the many buildings at Princeton, looking for the library's new location. Down a vast and deserted hallway, hanging up high, was the painting of a beautiful blonde girl holding a rose bloom to her lips.

Stunned, he froze in place, taking that painting in, breathing it, feeling the scent of that rose bloom, and reliving his darkest memories. His most treasured memories rekindled, he rejoiced in the image of the unknown girl who looked just like his sister. He stood there, captivated, unwilling to move and break the spell that had his blood rush through his veins like never before.

"It's been a while since I've met anyone who could be so transposed by art," a voice behind him interrupted.

Aggravated with the intrusion, he turned to face the stranger, his fists clenched hard and his joints crackling.

The man, who must've been at least sixty-five, extended his hand with a warm smile. "Allow me to introduce myself, young man. I'm Professor Timothy Joyce; I teach visual arts."

"Here?" David asked in disbelief.

"Yes, here," the professor laughed, patting him on the shoulder. "Don't tell me, you had no idea Princeton had a visual arts program?"

He shook his head, his eyes riveted on the girl in the painting, on her eyes, on the luscious lip touched by the rose petals. He wanted that... desperately.

"Can you... teach me?" he finally asked, transformed by an unbreakable spell.

He'd finally found his path in life.

He could learn how to recreate his dream girl, over and over again, looking for that elusive perfection, seeking a certain emotion in her eyes, putting it there somehow and reliving it every time he looked at his work. But most of all, he could anticipate the delayed gratification of the earth-shattering release he would feel when he'd find the perfect girl and immortalize her in a painting, for generations to come.

That fateful night, he shook Professor Joyce's hand once more. The following day, he dumped Nicole and changed his major to visual arts. Over the next three years, he worked side by side with the professor to cultivate his native talent with an obsessive pursuit of skill and mastery.

He was ready for his masterpiece.

12

CHIOCE

"You have to give me something," Tess shouted. "If we want to have the slightest chance to find this girl alive, I need an address now."

The unmarked SUV was still parked in front of the Bachert residence with its engine running, while the flow of freezing air coming from the vents did nothing to cool Tess's anger.

"Winnett, just understand that the man you have in your crosshairs is most likely not your perp," Donovan said, his voice still bearing the appearance of calm.

That methodical, unperturbed speech pattern fueled Tess's frustration. "Listen," she said, "this girl was entirely under this artist's spell. Have you seen this guy's paintings?"

"Yes, Winnett, I have seen David Bisset's paintings. I'm one of the million people who have. But he's one hundred percent clean. Doesn't even have a parking ticket. He's famous for showing his art but never selling it, that's the only weird stuff I was able to find out about him. While the PE teacher—"

"Screw the PE teacher," she reacted. "Kaylee had a rose in her bedroom and slept with the man's magazine cover pic on her night table, for crying out loud."

"And that makes him what? A kidnapper? Or a serial killer?" Donovan scoffed, and Tess uttered a long, detailed curse in response.

What made it worse was he had a point.

"He was dating a fifteen-year-old," Tess replied with the only piece of incriminating evidence she had against Bisset.

"Holding hands in that café. And he's what, thirty-six?"

"Yes, he's thirty-six," Donovan replied, a patient tone in his voice. "Look, all we know is he was *talking* with Kaylee, not dating her. She might've been in love with him and not the other way around. Hell, she could've fallen in love with his photo from the magazine. Teenage girl, hormones raging—"

"Or he could easily be what I believe he is. A predator who takes young girls and paints them. What he does afterwards with them I don't know yet. But here's a thought: can you run visual recognition on his paintings, see if we can identify who the models were?"

She heard a click, then Donovan's voice sounded differently when he spoke.

"That could take ages," he said. "Not to mention he could've painted those girls without real models, or using faces from fashion magazines, or something like that."

"You put me on speaker, didn't you?" she said, keeping her voice lower. Donovan's desk was in an open office space, and the last thing she wanted was for her raised voice to echo all over the floor.

"I did, yes," he admitted. "I had to put some distance between your voice and my brain," he added, then paused for a moment before continuing. "And I have Mr. Pearson—"

"And Pearson's there, right beside you?" she asked at the same time.

Donovan chuckled. "Great minds, Winnett."

She sighed, hiding an eyeroll, although Pearson couldn't see it.

"I'm hearing you have some leads," Pearson said. "Donovan's been telling me there's this teacher at Kaylee's school—"

"No offense, sir, but there's a rule that says you can't be

involved in the investigation of a missing family member."

There was a second of deathly silence on the line.

"I have to be, Winnett," Pearson said. "I really hope we won't get to the point where I have to pull rank."

"As you wish, as long as you remember you've been warned," Tess replied coldly.

"Winnett! What the hell is wrong with you?" her boss reacted.

"Bachert's already in line to have my badge when this is all over, and—"

"He already called, by the way," Pearson said.

"When?"

"Ten minutes ago. He mentioned something about you threatening his daughter, himself, bringing false and baseless accusations, using intimidation, and all that in the presence of his attorney. He demanded that you be removed from active duty pending a formal investigation."

Of course, he said all that, Tess thought, staring at the SUV's headliner. She decided it was best to not argue.

"I'm not all that surprised," Pearson said with an embittered sigh. "Did you get what you wanted?"

"Maybe," she replied cautiously. Pearson had reacted much worse in the past for the tiniest frown on the governor's forehead. "I have to choose between two leads. One is the logical, by-the-book suspect, this PE teacher. Donovan can fill you in."

"Yeah, his name is Milton Fuller, clear record, pays his taxes," Donovan said. "The only problem with Mr. Fuller is that until five years ago he didn't exist. Facial recognition identified him as Roger Potts, convicted pedophile from Wyoming. But for the other so-called suspect, we have nothing, not one single red flag, except Winnett's overactive gut."

"Winnett?" Pearson said, not needing to ask more.

"I say bust Fuller, send a team of locals to deal with him, but I'm willing to bet my life we won't find Kaylee with him."

"He was seen talking with the girls at the café," Donovan said.

"I need you to really hear me, D," she said. "This artist, Bisset, is our guy. Have you seen his paintings? Always young girls who could be sisters, always the rose. Did you notice the haunted, deathly look in their eyes? That's not art, D. That's a signature. A predator's signature. Dig deeper. Look at his childhood, school records, anything."

Donovan's fingers were dancing on the keyboard, while his mouth stayed shut. She'd touched a chord that had finally resonated with the analyst.

"Pedophiles never change age ranges," she continued her argument. "You know that. Pedophiles only care about girls under twelve, while Kaylee is fifteen. She was too old for your PE teacher. Let that one go and give me the damn address for David Bisset."

"Do it," she heard Pearson tell Donovan.

"Um, okay, but that's going to take me some time. Bisset has so many properties it's difficult to know where to send you. And what are you going to do without a warrant? No way you'll get one issued on the basis of the man's repetitive art."

"So, what, we can't find him?"

"We can," Donovan replied calmly. "It will take some doing, that's all. Usually, these rich people have their cellular accounts in someone else's name or use burners to protect their privacy. I'll run an analysis covering all his properties and see which cell numbers are common to those addresses. Then we'll find him."

He typed some more, while she waited.

"What do you think happened to Kaylee, Winnett?" Pearson asked, his voice heavy with worry.

She could barely hold on to the hope she'd still find her alive, and every passing minute made her even more frantic. Kaylee had been gone almost twenty-six hours, and a lot could happen to a girl like her in that amount of time, while at the whim of a predator.

"I'd rather not speculate, sir," she replied. "Let's stick to the facts we have and find her as soon as we can. That's all that matters."

"I got something," Donovan announced. "Might be something, might not be. I peeked into a sealed therapy record for David Bisset. When he was eleven, his sister Aimée drowned in the family pool. Seems that he accidentally witnessed the mortician prepare his sister's body and was shocked, or something. Says here he underwent therapy for a year and made a complete and successful recovery."

"That was his trigger," Winnett said. "Is there anything else?"

"Probably not. His parents' plane crashed when he was eighteen years old."

"Any changes in his life after that event?"

"Nothing for about two years, when he shifted his major to art and became reclusive."

"This is our guy, Donovan, I'm telling you. It's right there, staring you in the eye. Trigger event during childhood years, reclusive behavior, displayed obsessions, almost like a twisted form of exhibitionism. What else do you need?"

"You're scary, Winnett, did I ever tell you that?"

"I'll get even scarier if I don't have a bloody address in five seconds."

She thought about David Bisset for a moment, staring at his photo on the cover of *Art Review*. In the background, one of his paintings, a large canvas hung above the mantle of a smoke-darkened fireplace. Who was that girl? What would someone like him do with the girl, once the paintings were completed?

"How come none of these girls have ever stepped forward to make their claim to fame as Bisset's models?" she asked, thinking out loud.

"Jeez, Winnett," Pearson said.

"I really wish you didn't have to hear this next part, sir."

"Spill it, already."

"Okay," she replied quietly, after a split-second hesitation. Her boss knew all the sinister facts of their profession. Whatever scenario she could think of, whatever monsters she'd seen, he'd seen them too. "Donovan, please run a missing person search with the following parameters: girls eleven to sixteen, who have disappeared from this area since David Bisset turned reclusive. Then run a visual comparison between the girls in the paintings and the missing girls' cases that are still open." She paused for a moment, thinking if what she wanted was possible. "He's a talented artist; we should be able to see the resemblance."

"On it," he replied. "The system will probably choke on the paintings, but I'll do it by hand. They're only... twenty-eight," he added, his voice down to a chilling whisper as he spoke the numbers.

"Well, if you find a few matches, that will get us a warrant. Until then, I'll just knock politely and interview the son of a bitch."

13

THE FIRST

David's first painting that was not part of school curriculum had been an exulting experience.

He'd been timid at first, afraid to tell the model what he was looking for, what he wanted her to do. But the girl, one of the many nameless runaway kids who beat street corners, was eagerly looking to please him, especially since he'd shown her a wad of cash thicker than her chain-strapped purse.

Without a word, she'd stripped naked and lay on the bed just as he'd told her to, hands crossed on her chest, and endured while he adorned her body with countless roses. She must've been happy to just sit there and wait, while he arranged the setting. The alternative, considering the young girl's chosen profession, would've probably been to satisfy a balding, pot-bellied truck driver in some dark parking lot who'd gasp hoarsely and swear while she finished the job as quickly as she could.

Then he'd lowered the thermostat setting, bringing the temperature inside the studio to sixty-five, hoping to bring a bluish tint to the girl's alabaster skin. It didn't work too well, because his hands also froze and turned stiff, and the quality of his work suffered.

He found himself struggling with the very experience he'd eagerly anticipated and planned in the finest detail. The arousal wasn't there; something critical was missing, and his painting was uninspired, redolent of work done for hire and in a hurry.

But then he remembered the blood coming out of Aimée's vein, what he'd felt when he'd seen it, and decided to add that thrill to his well-rehearsed scenario. He lacked the proper tools and skills for it; turned out phlebotomy was not as easy as he'd imagined. The girl, who'd initially agreed to the bloodletting, had started screaming and writhing, seeing how badly he was botching the job, and he had no other choice but to silence her with a hard blow across the face.

Out of breath after fighting her, he stopped and looked at her, his body shaking, at first from effort and adrenaline, then from an intense and thrilling lust. Her body, splayed naked and vulnerable among hundreds of roses, a rivulet of blood leaving her still body and staining her pale skin, her flesh, cold to the touch, her eyes, closed into eternity... it was as if he was eleven years old again, back in that room at the mortuary, alone with Aimée, no one to know what he had done.

His body shaking with excitement, he rushed to his mother's bedroom, maintained intact after her death, and got her makeup kit. He touched up the girl's skin, covering the traces of the blows he'd landed.

She never woke up.

He worked frenetically and finished the painting in a few hours, sexual tension building with each brush stroke. When it was finished, the painting was breathtaking, and he was ready for his craved release.

He only wished she could've fought him off some more, when he possessed her frozen body.

As the sun rose and engulfed the studio in unforgiving rays of light, he realized he still had work to do. Completing his first painting had been exhilarating, but he could do better. Striving for a higher high, like all addicts, David started planning every move carefully, obsessively.

He turned to his two-acre rose garden with renewed interest.

That morning, he carefully overturned a certain rose bed, so that the plants wouldn't suffer, removed some of the black soil, and replaced it with the girl's body. Then he set the rose bed back in its place, seemingly untouched, and spread the remaining soil throughout the garden. The gardeners who tended to the vast property wouldn't notice a single thing out of place.

Over the following weeks, he noticed how those particular rose bushes were growing faster and blooming richer and more scented than any other rose, the decaying nourishment at the tips of their roots feeding them richly, the girl's essence now running through rose petal veins. Fascinated, David walked through the garden every day, spending hours staring at the blooms, touching them, smelling them, visualizing the subject of his next portrait.

Only next time, he'd start from a rose bush, not from a girl. He'd choose the final resting place of his model first, then use roses from that particular rose bed to adorn her body. He'd make sure the subject's makeup would reflect the color of that rose mixed in with the fascinating, captivating color of blood.

His first painting soon became famous, and private collectors from around the globe offered millions of dollars for it. Yet he never considering selling it; the girl was his forever. But there was a part of him that wanted the world to know what he'd done, to be in awe of his mastery. He wanted to show everyone what he could do, so he promoted his work in galleries and museums. And the world smiled back. Not only was he one of the most desirable bachelors out there, rich and handsome and incredibly successful, but he was also a very talented artist. Art lovers, collectors, and critics talked about his first portrait for months, wondering what the mesmerizing expression in the girl's eyes could've been about.

Not knowing they were wondering about eyes that had been drained of any expression when life had left her body. Not knowing he'd had to glue her eyelids open to finish painting her.

What an unfortunate mistake, that girl dying too early on him.

Once he knew exactly what he wanted, he devised a new plan. He was going to be in total control.

14

STUDIO

Tess approached Bisset's address quietly. She'd turned off the lights and siren as soon as she entered the neighborhood. She parked alongside the property's west fence, after passing in front the closed, wrought-iron gates and turning the corner.

She approached the thick, luxurious hedge and peeked inside the yard. There was no one in sight, no activity, no lights on, no cars parked in the small lot tucked at the side of the house, where probably the staff parked their cars.

Yet Donovan had reassured her that the cell phone most likely to belong to David Bisset was pinging active inside that property. She brought up the map on her phone and visualized the property layout. Splayed on five acres of lush gardens and tropical shrubs and trees, the single-story stone mansion imposed with large windows, a circular driveway, and white marble steps leading to the main entrance.

Palm trees were planted toward the edges of the property to confer privacy to the residents. Closer to the house, the lawn was clear, a perfectly trimmed, emerald green surface still sparkling droplets of sprinkler water in the sun.

Tess walked along the west edge of the property toward the back, stopping every few yards to take another look. The house seemed engulfed in silence and darkness, most of its windows covered to keep the sun out. If David Bisset was in there and had Kaylee, he was busy doing whatever the hell he was doing to her and probably didn't want to be disturbed. Would ringing the doorbell precipitate what Tess was trying to prevent?

She checked the time again; Kaylee had been missing for twenty-eight hours already. There was no more time to waste on maybes.

She drove back to the main gate and pressed the intercom buzzer. No one answered. She pressed it again, longer. Still nothing.

She got out of the SUV and approached the gate. It was controlled by an electric motor and designed to open inward on wheels. She wished for a lock she could easily pick. Instead, she had to open a massive gate secured in place with the power of electricity. No amount of her physical strength would pry it open enough.

She took a small wire cutter from her vehicle's toolbox, then found the steel wire that pulled the gate shut and held it in place. It took a bit of doing, but soon the steel cable snapped and snaked inertly to the ground, and the left side of the gate became loose, just enough for her to get inside.

From there, she rushed to the front door and rang the bell insistently.

She didn't have to wait much.

The door swung open and David Bisset smiled inquisitively, a shadow of a frown on his forehead.

"Yes?"

With him came the smell of fresh oil paint and solvent, carried over on a wave of chilly, moist air escaping the confines of the house. He wore paint-stained jeans and an originally white T-shirt and was wiping his hands on a paint-stained rag.

She flashed her badge quickly, then put her wallet back in her pocket.

"David Bisset?" she asked, although she recognized him from the *Art Review* cover photo.

"That's me," he replied, and his smile widened. No question came about how she'd bypassed the front gate.

In person, his charisma was intoxicating. Tess had expected to feel something in his presence, something troublesome, a gut feeling telling her she was in the presence of a predator. Instead, she was painfully aware she was gawking at the superb exemplar of the human species.

Leopards are just as beautiful, she thought. *Deadly too.*

"I have a few questions for you," she said. "Mind if we take this out of the heat?"

He invited her inside with a wide gesture, then closed the door behind her. The thud of massive oak hitting the frame brought a chill to her spine. Her gut was finally talking to her.

The living room was huge, but kept almost completely dark by roller shades controlled by a centralized motor, because all of them had been lowered to precisely the same height, allowing only a few inches of light to come in. The theme of the room was dark also, from the mahogany hardwood to the walnut and burgundy leather furniture.

The ceiling was high, at least sixteen feet, and on the walls, his world-famous paintings hung one next to the other, all the same size, but all different. The girls were different, and so were the roses. She gazed quickly around the room, counting thirty-two of them; Donovan must've been wrong, or maybe Bisset hadn't yet showed some of his canvases to the public.

She gazed quickly at Bisset. He was waiting patiently, a smile still fluttering on his lips. He seemed flattered by her attention, soaking in her amazement, her reactions to seeing his art up-close. The photos she'd seen in the art magazines weren't doing the paintings much justice. From a few feet away, those girls seemed alive, staring at her from their life-size portraits and sending shivers down her spine.

She took a few steps toward the fireplace. The painting that had hung above the marble mantle had been lowered and was leaning against the wall, leaving an empty space above the fireplace.

"Thank you for allowing me the time to admire your work," Tess said eventually, wondering if the place above the mantle had been reserved for Kaylee's portrait.

"My pleasure," he replied, inviting her with a gesture to take a seat.

She ignored his invitation and remained standing in front of the fireplace.

"What can I do for you, Agent, um—"

"Winnett," she replied. "We're investigating the disappearance of Kaylee Lewis. Do you know her, Mr. Bisset?"

He hesitated for a split second, then replied calmly, showing no sign of deceit. "N—no, can't say that I do."

"And yet we have you on tape, speaking with her at Café Dream," Tess replied, showing him her phone.

He reached out as if to take the phone from her hand but seeing how she withdrew, he mumbled an apology and leaned to look at it instead. While he studied the grainy photo, Tess noticed a red stain on his right index finger. *Blood,* she thought. *Or is it paint? Am I losing my mind here?*

"Oh, her," he reacted calmly. "Yes, I have spoken with her a couple of times. I asked her to pose for me. She said no. End of story."

She studied him intently, seeking the tiniest microexpressions that would show signs of deception. There was nothing, and for that, there could only be one explanation.

David Bisset was a true psychopath. One who showed

absolutely no remorse and no fear, one whose heart rate wouldn't rise when cornered by a cop like her.

"Do you know where Kaylee might've gone after you spoke with her two days ago? We're trying to reconstruct the last day before she disappeared," she said, keeping her tone friendly and relaxed.

He leaned against the mantle, touching it with his right index finger. Some of that red stain smudged the white marble.

He smiled again, a mesmerizing smile that showed two lines of perfectly white teeth but didn't touch his eyes. "I'm sorry, I have no idea. If you don't need anything else—"

"Do you ever sell your art?" she asked, cutting him off before he could ask her to leave. Legally, once she'd been asked to leave, she had to comply. Her instinct told her he'd be eager to talk about his art, even with her.

"No," he replied, his smile widening and touching his eyes. "I don't have to. Isn't it wonderful to be the exception to the broke artist cliché?"

"And this?" she pointed at the painting that probably once hung above the mantle.

His smile waned. "Sometimes I shuffle things around. It's my idea of redecorating the place. I'm planning to replace this painting with another. Soon."

There was tension in his jaws as he spoke.

"Something new?" she asked, feigning adulating enthusiasm. "Could I see it, please?"

"No... I'm sorry, I never show anyone my work before it's finished. And now, please excuse me, I'm busy, and my paints will dry out."

"Sure, I understand," she replied quickly. "Before I go, could I possibly trouble someone for a glass of water?" she asked, as if assuming he had staff. Mansions of that size always had.

He let out a quiet groan of frustration. "I'll get it," he said, then vanished out of sight.

Tess took out her keys. Attached to the key ring, she carried a small flashlight equipped with a UV LED light. The room was dark enough to allow the small beam of light to identify whether that stain on the mantle was blood or paint. In UV light, blood turned dark, black almost, while other bodily fluids fluoresced.

She turned the flashlight on and ran its beam over that smudge, but it didn't change color. She ran it again over the sides of the fireplace or other surfaces he might've touched with his stained finger. Nothing turned dark, nothing lit up either.

Getting ready to leave while her gut screamed she should stay, she relaxed her hand before turning the flashlight off. In its path, the beam touched the surface of the painting that leaned against the wall, by her side. Sections of it turned black under the UV light. There was blood mixed in with the paint, and now she had evidence.

She turned off the beam, considering her options. She could take him down and search the premises. Maybe Kaylee was still alive, even if the mansion was eerily quiet. The complete absence of house staff was also a bad sign. If Kaylee had been nothing but his underage lover, visiting under her own volition, the house staff, sworn to secrecy, would've probably been still allowed to do their jobs.

But what if she searched the premises and did not find anyone? He'd never say another word, and Kaylee would be forever lost, dying or dead already, wherever he was holding her.

She could leave now and come back with support. Arrest him, but for what charges? Then hope to question him and break him. However, her experience working with psychopaths told her that was an unlikely scenario; David Bisset would never talk, his overpriced attorneys making sure of that within moments of his arrest. And the blood in the painting, fruit of the poisonous tree of her unwarranted stay on the premises after he'd repeatedly asked her to leave, would be thrown out of court in an equally short amount of time.

But did Kaylee still have time? What if Tess's visit had spooked him? Would Bisset wait for Tess to finally leave and rush to kill the girl and hide her body before Tess could come back with a warrant?

When Bisset reappeared with a tall glass of water, she thanked him with a nod and took the glass.

"I have to leave," Tess replied, planning to leave the house for a moment, enough to text Donovan her findings, but then return and search the premises. She felt it in her gut, in her entire being that Kaylee was there, and she was willing to do whatever it took to find her alive. "I received an urgent message from work," she explained, placing the glass on the mantle.

That moment, her phone chimed, and she chuckled apologetically, then took her eyes off Bisset to look at the screen.

A message from Donovan said, "Fourteen matches found. Warrant in progress."

She typed quickly, "Send backup now," but didn't get to tap send.

Something hit her in the back of her head, and she collapsed, seeing stars before her universe turned dark.

15

MONSTER

Everything was dark and deathly quiet. Tess forced her eyes open, but her vision was clouded by a fog of blackness against which sparks of green shone brightly. When those subsided, she heard herself moan as she put her hands under her body, trying to lift herself up.

Her vision started to return slowly, at first as a faint light allowing her to barely distinguish the largest pieces of furniture from the rest of the space, then to see the light coming from the phone's screen, down on the floor, a few feet away. She crawled over there, the throbbing in her head blinding her with every heartbeat. Before she could reach it, Bisset's foot came down on it hard, smashing it to pieces.

She took her hand to her weapon holster, only to find it empty.

"Looking for this?" Bisset showed her something she couldn't distinguish in the prevailing darkness, then cackled, a loud laughter that sent echoes in the vast room.

Before she slipped away, she chanted in her mind, "Donovan knows I'm here. Donovan knows I'm here."

When she came to, she didn't recognize the place. She wasn't in Bisset's living room anymore. The light was blindingly bright, driving sharp blades into her throbbing head. She lay on her back, unable to move. She tried harder, while her frantic eyes searched the room looking for a way out, registering every detail.

The first thing she noticed was Kaylee, still alive, lying only two feet away on a leather bed and surrounded by roses. She was pale and barely conscious, while blood dripped from her vein and collected in a china bowl, but she was alive, nevertheless. Tess tried to smile at the girl, but the horror written on Kaylee's face withered her smile. She followed Kaylee's gaze to find a frenzied, transfigured Bisset painting with almost furious moves, every few minutes rushing over near them to study something, to scrutinize them with cold, intense eyes.

Tess felt dizzy and nauseated; she realized she'd been drugged, but the effects were starting to wear off. She tried to lift her arms again but realized she'd been tied up, the thought sending waves of horror and unwanted memories to her panicked mind, memories of a night twelve years ago when she'd been assaulted and barely made it out alive.

She tugged more forcefully at the restraints and felt a pinch in her arm. When she realized why, it took all her willpower to keep her from screaming. A needle had been stuck into her vein, and blood was trickling through a tube into another china bowl.

She took deep breaths and focused on trying to control the waves of sheer panic coursing through her. Images of her haunted past, that man's hands on her skin, the excruciating pain when he cut her, his weight suffocating her. She squeezed her eyes shut, forcing the unwanted memory to disappear. "I survived you," she muttered to the monster of her past, "and then I killed you. I put you into the ground, where you belong."

She took one more breath of air, then opened her eyes. "And I'll survive this one."

Her panic subsided; her lucid reasoning returned in full force. She took a few seconds to observe Bisset's pattern and to calculate her next steps. When he was absorbed in his work with his face hidden behind the canvas, she tugged at the restraints holding her wrists immobilized, but this time paying attention on how the tension felt, how much slack they seemed to have.

The right wrist's cuff seemed a little looser, and she decided to favor that. Slowly, without sudden movements that could've alerted Bisset, she forced her hand to squeeze through the leather restraint, one millimeter at a time, painfully slow, until it was free. Then she undid the tie from her left cuff but didn't move her arm. She let her right arm settle along her body as if still tied up and called out.

"It must be exhilarating to have the opportunity to paint both of us, isn't it, David?" she asked.

Kaylee writhed, whispering, "No, please don't. Please be quiet."

Bisset looked at her briefly from behind the canvas but didn't engage.

"Only a true artist would try what you're doing here today," Tess continued, playing on his narcissistic strings like a violin in the moonlight. "You've never tried this before, have you?"

He scowled at her. "Shut the hell up," he said, but continued to work frenetically.

"Can you imagine what people will say when they see your biggest masterpiece ever?" she asked, taking a deep breath, steeling herself. "Everyone knows the girl with a rose is Aimée, and everyone knows how you feel about her. People have been talking, you know, about you, Aimée, and what happened that night in the mortuary."

The sound of a paintbrush forcefully hitting the window brought a flicker of a smile on Tess's lips. Unable to lift her throbbing head much, she listened for his approaching footfalls.

"Shut the fuck up," he shouted, only inches away from her face.

Without blinking, she drew breath and punched him in the throat with all the strength she could muster. He choked and faltered back a few steps until he reached the wall, both his hands frantically feeling his throat where it hurt, trying to find what was broken.

"I bet your erection is gone now, huh?" Tess said, quickly pulling the needle from her vein and removing her ankle cuffs. She rushed to Kaylee's side, and took the needle from her vein, then started to undo her restraints, throwing the roses on the floor.

A terrified moan coming from Kaylee's pale lips got Tess to turn around, just when Bisset was lunging at her with both fists clenched.

"Don't touch her," he spoke in a coarse yet forceful voice. "You're ruining everything."

She managed to move out of his path, but she was still weak, dizzy, unsure on her feet. She tripped against the edge of an area rug and fell hard, sending waves of agonizing pain through her body when her head hit the floor. She twisted and writhed away just in time to avoid his heavy foot and backtracked under a table to escape his kicks.

Desperate, she looked around for something to use as a weapon. She pulled herself out from underneath the table, ignoring the throbbing in her head, and made for the fireplace, where pokers were waiting, neatly arranged in a holder.

She heard a roar of anger as he attacked again and knew she didn't have much left in her. Feeling she was about to faint, she barely reached the fireplace when a familiar sight caught her eye. Right there, inches away, on the mantle, was her service weapon.

She always carried a round chambered, safety off.

She took aim and fired, just as he was lunging again, fists clenched and a terrifying grimace on his face.

He fell into a heap, crushing her under his heavy body.

"And I'll put you in the ground too, where you belong," she whispered, struggling to extricate herself from under his weight.

When she could stand, she rushed to Kaylee and checked her vitals. Her pulse was weak, but her weary heart was still beating. She covered the girl's body with a sheet, whispering words of reassurance, just as she heard the door being broken down by the SWAT team.

"In here," she called weakly, holding Kaylee's hand in hers.

Pearson was the first man in, followed by Donovan.

"Get a bus," she said, "tell them to be ready for an emergency transfusion."

As in a dream, she heard Donovan make the call, and saw Pearson talking to Kaylee, who'd opened her eyes. And then she saw nothing else but darkness, but this time it wasn't scary anymore. She welcomed it.

She woke up living a nightmare. She was immobilized, couldn't move her arms, and each time she tried to free her arm, she felt the poke of a needle stuck in her vein. She screamed.

"Whoa, easy now, Winnett," she heard Donovan say. "It's all right, you're all right."

She stared at him, blinking away tears of unspeakable fear. He was smiling. Pearson was right there too. She breathed, the familiar sight of the people she trusted shattering her panic, and realized she was on a stretcher, next to an ambulance.

"Let me go," she said, her eyes still throwing panic-tinted glances at everyone around her.

"Ma'am, you have to lie back and rest," a young EMS technician ordered in the voice he probably used on children.

"The hell I do," she replied. "Let. Me. Go."

The EMS technician sighed and looked at Pearson, who nodded his approval. He removed the stretcher straps. "You have a concussion, and you've lost some blood," he said. "You have to report to the ER today. Not tomorrow, today."

"This too," she said, pointing at the needle piercing her vein.

"This is just fluids to help—"

"Off."

He removed the needle and put a Band-Aid where the needle had been.

Tess got off the stretcher, leaning against Donovan's arm.

"Who would've known," he said laughing, "the mighty Winnett screaming like a damsel in distress."

She turned to him and grabbed him by the lapels. "One word about this to anyone and I'll—"

She didn't finish her sentence, because Deanne Lewis rushed over and hugged her so tightly it took the air out of her lungs.

"Thank you," the woman whispered through tears, "thank you for finding my baby."

She hugged her back, tightly, thinking how much she appreciated the warmth of another human being after staring into a horrible abyss the entire day.

She walked with Deanne to where the EMS techs were loading Kaylee in the ambulance. They had her on a large-bore transfusion, and she was awake. Tess squeezed the girl's hand, shivering when her cold skin touched hers. "You'll be okay, kiddo," she managed to say before they loaded the stretcher into the ambulance.

Tess watched the bus roll away, then noticed another familiar face watching her. Seated in the back of a black SUV, Governor Bachert watched every move she made with a deep frown on his forehead.

"You're not going to believe this, Winnett," Donovan said, appearing out of nowhere, while she kept her gaze focused on Bachert. "You were right. The team brought cadaver dogs, and they're finding grave after grave in the rose garden from hell. How did you know?"

Yeah... she'd been right. She was always right about the twisted mind games of serial killers.

But she'd hesitated. Would she have hesitated to break down the door of a different unsub? Less rich, less powerful? Her hesitation could've costed Kaylee her life. And she'd made another mistake, a big one. She'd taken her eyes off the man whom she believed was a serial killer to check her text messages, and *that* almost cost her Kaylee's life, in addition to her own.

"What the hell is wrong with you, Winnett?" she muttered, leaving Donovan in place, slack-jawed, as she walked toward the governor's car.

Maybe Bachert was right. Maybe she didn't have what it took to do the job. Not anymore.

She pulled out her wallet with a wince of pain shooting arrows through her right shoulder, then extracted her badge and offered it to the man.

"To save you the trouble, sir."

Bachert gave her a long stare, then said, "Not on your life, Winnett." Then he tapped on the door twice, and the driver set the SUV in motion.

She stared after the departing SUV until it disappeared from view, then started walking back toward the house. Her entire body ached. Maybe lying down wouldn't be such a bad idea after all.

"Winnett," Pearson called, and she went to meet him.

They stood side by side in silence and watched as Bisset's body was loaded into the coroner's van. The technicians slammed the doors shut, and shortly thereafter, the van set in motion.

As the van passed by them, Pearson turned toward her and said, with a barely visible glint of pride in his eyes, "You had to shoot this one too, didn't you, Winnett?"

Did *Girl With A Rose* keep you riveted to the pages as you raced through the story, gasping at every twist? Find out what happens next for Tess Winnett and her team, in the next unmissable Leslie Wolfe thriller.

Read on for previews from:

Mile High Death
An absolutely enthralling crime thriller novella.

*** and ***

A Beautiful Couple

He's a charismatic TV anchor with everything to lose. She's the perfect wife, desperate to protect their life. But after one fatal mistake, their picture-perfect world starts to unravel.

Thank You!

A big, heartfelt thank you for choosing to read my book. If you enjoyed it, please take a moment to leave me a four or five-star review; I would be very grateful. It doesn't need to be more than a couple of words, and it makes a huge difference.

Join my mailing list to receive special offers, exclusive bonus content, and news about upcoming new releases. Use the button below, visit www.LeslieWolfe.com to sign up, or email me at LW@WolfeNovels.com.

Did you enjoy *Girl With a Rose*? Would you like to see some of these characters return? Which ones? Your thoughts and feedback are very valuable to me. Please contact me directly through one of the channels listed below. Email works best: LW@WolfeNovels.com or use the button below:

If you haven't already, check out *Dawn Girl*, a gripping, heart stopping crime thriller and the first book in the Tess Winnett series. If you enjoyed *Criminal Minds*, you'll enjoy *Dawn Girl*. Or, if you're in a mood for something lighter, try ***Las Vegas Girl***; you'll love it.

CONNECT WITH ME

a, Amazon.com/LeslieWolfe

✉ LW@WolfeNovels.com

a, Amazon.com/stores/Leslie-Wolfe/author/B00KR1QZ0G

🌐 LeslieWolfe.com

f Facebook.com/wolfenovels

📷 Instagram.com/Wolfe.Leslie

♪ TikTok.com/@Leslie.Wolfe

B Bookbub.com/authors.leslie-wolfe

1

FLIGHT

Her heart swelled as she stepped on the heated tarmac. She almost didn't look at the cabbie, while the old and disapproving crab handed her the wheelie with the laptop bag affixed on top. His watery eyes shifted from her beaming smile to her slim figure and then to the slick Gulfstream G650ER waiting with the cabin door open. The sight of the business jet brought out a scoff, followed shortly by a clucking of his tongue, none of which he made the tiniest effort to disguise.

Her smile withered just a tiny bit. She hated being judged by anyone, more so by this cog in the transportation machine, someone who, if he didn't watch it, risked forfeiting his tip.

"Anything wrong?" she asked, ready to give him a piece of her mind in a tone he'd remember for a while, even if it seemed he'd already started grappling with senility.

He just scoffed again and extended his hand, anticipating payment for his service. She obliged, shaking her head slowly, and deciding she wasn't going to let him ruin her mood. Who did he think he was, judging her like that? How did he know that jet wasn't hers to begin with?

She breathed with ease the moment he drove off, leaving her alone on the tarmac, wheelie handle in hand, only some forty yards from the idling plane.

Her beaming smile returned in full force.

She couldn't believe what was happening to her. Experiences like these never happened to girls from Rapid City, Iowa. Only yesterday, after yet another endless sales presentation conducted under the fierce eyes of her boss and the initially indifferent looks of the client, she'd thought she'd have to return to Miami crammed in an economy seat by her boss's side, enduring crappy conversation, spiced with occasional lewdness and permanent halitosis.

But no . . . a late-night delivery of flowers and champagne, delivered in white gloves straight to her hotel room, had accompanied a handwritten note on luscious white cardstock.

"Experience life my way," the note read, and she mused over each letter, breathing in the words that brought butterflies to her stomach.

The white-gloved man waited respectfully by the door, and when she looked up from the note, he delivered his instructions.

She was invited to fly home to Miami in Richard's personal jet, departing from the Houston Executive Airport at noon, or whenever she'd like. Due to concerns for his privacy and to keep the media vampires at bay, she was kindly asked to wear a hat and sunglasses on her way to the airport and refrain from speaking to anyone about the invitation. Mr. Sanford would be delighted to share Miss Lambert's company. He was also regretful he could not join her for dinner that night. Nevertheless, he had made arrangements for her and would be thrilled if she would say yes.

She couldn't find words; her throat, constricted by emotion, barely allowed her to nod and utter her approval. Then she quickly grabbed her purse and checked her looks in the mirror.

Enchanted, she followed the young man downstairs to the restaurant, stepping quickly and quietly on her stilettos, the sound of her heels smothered by the plush carpeting of the luxury hotel. She was surprised that Brad, her boss, had sprung for such a nice stay; probably he'd matched their travel budget with the size of the prospect he was trying to impress.

The man held the door for her as she entered Mastro's Steakhouse, an exquisite culinary landmark she didn't have a travel budget for. It didn't seem to matter, when she was led directly by a smiling hostess to an entire area that had been cordoned off, keeping curious guests at bay.

A single table was set on an impeccable, white damask cloth, a white rose in a tall, crystal vase marking its center. Another card leaned against the thin, tall cylinder.

"Myra, have dinner with me," the card read, *"at least in spirit if not in person. Until tomorrow, we can only dream."*

Her moist eyes lingered on the letters spelling her name. He had a way with words, she had to admit. He was unparalleled at making a girl feel special, and she'd almost forgotten she'd overheard Richard order three dozen roses for his wife as a wedding anniversary gift. Okay, so he wasn't going to be hers forever; he was married. Bummer . . . but still.

She stopped reminiscing and filled her lungs with the hot and humid air, loaded with hints of jet fuel and exhaust, and the scent of sweltering asphalt under the summer sun. She approached the jet, wondering what the trip would be like. How Richard would be.

She was ten yards from the plane's door when he appeared at the top of the steps, as breathtaking as she remembered him from yesterday's excruciating overview of Southeast Chemical and Paper product offering and special terms for high-volume contracts.

There was a ruggedness to his handsome features, an intensity in his eyes that brought butterflies to her stomach, anticipating the moment he'd touch her skin, leaving searing traces where his fingers would wander. When their eyes met, a spark traveled through her entire body and stretched her lips in an excited smile. She playfully tilted her head to the side and stopped, waiting for him to close the distance.

As he did, his eyes tensed, while traveling her body from head to toe and back. He lingered a little where the hem of her tight skirt touched her thighs, then found the curves of her full breasts, where the silk of her white blouse exposed her tan skin.

Without a word, he grabbed the handle of her wheelie, his eyes locked with hers, intense, a sense of dire urgency conveyed in the directness of the gaze, so dire it prickled her skin with goosebumps and brought a flicker of a frown to her forehead.

She followed him, nevertheless, her hand melting in his firm grip, letting him lead her aboard the idling aircraft.

"Where would you like me to sit?" she asked, finding herself flustered and hesitant all of a sudden, an unfamiliar feeling for her. She'd always been brave, unyielding, determined. That's how she made it out of Iowa and had built a life for herself in Miami, as an account executive for a Fortune 500 company. But this man had a perplexing effect on her. She seemed to be subdued entirely to his will, as if she'd lost the ability to think for herself somewhere between the flower and champagne delivery last night and the solo dinner that had followed.

He closed the aircraft door and locked it, then laughed, turning to face her. He grabbed her hand with a playful smile that didn't reach his tense, dark eyes.

"It's just the two of us, so, wherever you like."

She swallowed, feeling wary, as a chill traveled down her spine.

"How about the pilot?" she asked.

"You're looking at him," he replied, his low voice eager, the same urgency coming across in the way the words were spoken. "Why don't you join me in the cockpit?"

Her full-bloom smile returned, while her uneasiness dissipated. She'd never seen the inside of a jet's cockpit before.

She followed his lead and took a seat by his side. He fastened her seatbelt, his hands brushing against her body and sending waves of excitement through her heated skin. He helped her put on her headset, his fingers getting caught in her long, wavy hair. Not by accident, she was sure, and the thought of that brought another round of butterflies, just as he was getting cleared for takeoff by the Houston Executive Airport tower.

"You've completely ruined commercial flying for me," she said playfully. "How will I ever be able to do my job, flying economy at least two times a week?"

He just grinned, looking at her for a long, loaded moment. Then he refocused on his controls, flying the plane without a word. Tension had tightly clenched his jaws, muscles knotting under his skin. She wondered why. There was something off about him, his reactions to seeing her, to her being there with him, in that tight space, all alone with him in the sky.

He touched a few controls, and then released the buckle of his seatbelt.

"Autopilot's on, and we're free to move around the cabin," he said, his voice a bit colder than she'd heard him speak to her in her dreams.

She followed him toward the back of the plane and managed to smile when he offered her a glass of champagne.

She dipped her lips in the chilled liquid. "How long is the flight?"

He abandoned his glass on the small table and touched her

hair. "Long enough," he replied with a waning smile. He took the glass from her hand and led her to the back of the plane, her hand numb in his tight grip. When he stopped and looked at her, his gaze chilled the blood in her veins. His eyes were cold, dark, and lusting with an intensity she hadn't seen before. For a brief and illogical moment, she thought of screaming and running away, but who would hear her, and where would she go?

Somehow, between yesterday's magic and today's reality, her dream had turned into a nightmare.

She forced her lungs to draw air and her hands to stop shaking.

He opened the door to a rear compartment that had been lushly decorated as an inflight bedroom and led her inside, his grip on her hand just as merciless, his gaze intensifying with unspoken menace.

She tried to pull back, but he easily held her in place, not releasing her wrist. The corners of his mouth flickered with a smirk as his left hand gently caressed her long, dark hair, softly playing with the curls, while his eyes drilled into hers.

"Please," she whimpered, too scared to think straight. "I—"

He grabbed a fistful of her hair and pulled down forcefully, forcing her head back. Then he ripped her blouse off with a quick gesture, leaning over her with a grin of lustful and merciless anticipation.

She screamed until her lungs were empty of air, then drew breath and let out another shriek, her wails covered by the jet engines and his laughter.

"You and I are going to have so much fun, my darling Gen," he said, undoing his zipper. "You'll finally get what you really want."

Stunned, she stared into his deathly eyes. "My name's not—"

He slapped her hard across the face. He licked his lips as he watched her eyes tear up and the blood stain her swollen mouth. He tasted that bit of redness while his hands traveled lower on her body, unyielding.

"Oh, my darling, *darling* Gen," he whispered in her ear, his voice menacing, an evil foreboding that chilled her to the bone. "I've been dreaming of this moment since the day I met you."

Against all reason, she screamed.

2

BODY

Tess approached the cordoned-off area with a raised eyebrow and muttered oaths, quickly making her way past the emergency vehicles with the flashers on, through dozens of onlookers and media people frantic to get a quote or a shot of the victim, anything to fuel the masses' lust for blood and sensation. A couple of news helicopters were circling the area, always hungry buzzards eager for some fodder.

"Agent Winnett," a familiar voice called from the crowd. "Tess!"

She stopped and turned, searching the crowd for the face that went with that voice.

"Mr. Rusch," she acknowledged the man holding a microphone with a local TV station's logo. "You've moved up in the world, I see. You switched from investigative journalism to the world of fake and scandalous drama," she added, unable to refrain from smiling.

"A man's gotta eat," he replied unfazed. "But my heart is and always will be in investigative journalism," he added, lowering the foam-padded microphone. "Which is why I have to ask, what's going on here?"

She touched his shoulder briefly in a gesture of camaraderie. They went back years, and on occasions, he'd proven helpful and a good resource to have by her side. "I'll tell you everything I know so far." She paused, giving him time to start his camera, while a glint of amusement lit her eyes. "I woke up, had my coffee, and got called to assist with a new investigation."

"Wait . . . What? That's it?"

"I just got here, Mr. Rusch. And I'm not psychic."

Deflated, the man lowered his camera and ran a weary hand against his receding hairline. "I thought you were down with calling me Brandt."

"Okay, Brandt, but I still don't have anything else to share. Now, will you please excuse me?" She walked away quickly, waving off the approaching horde of frustrated journalists.

Tess flashed her FBI badge, and the Collier County deputy posted by the perimeter lifted the yellow tape with a quick head nod. She slowed her pace, allowing herself time to take in the details.

A wide section of the Naples beach had been cordoned off, keeping all tourists at bay. A few yards from the shore, a Coast Guard vessel had dropped anchor, and several Coasties were getting ready to bring a body to shore. Waist deep in clear, turquoise waters, Doc Rizza instructed them in a loud, slightly raspy voice.

Tess put her hand up to shield her eyes from the piercing sun. In the distance, bright red Coast Guard helicopters were flying in a search pattern. If she squinted hard, to the point of tearing up, she could make out several WaveRunners searching the waters, also in a search pattern.

There was another vessel at anchor, as close to shore as it could possibly reach, a fifty-foot yacht with two people onboard and an incessantly barking retriever pacing the deck. The woman had wrapped herself in a blanket, despite the afternoon heat, and the man stood by her side in a protective stance, as if the Coast Guard and all the law enforcement swarming on the beach were a dire and immediate threat to their lives.

"Hey," she heard a man say, "thanks for coming."

She shook the hand extended and then hugged the Palm Beach County detective. "Boy, did you wake up on the wrong side of the peninsula today or what?" she asked, stepping back and looking at him with scrutinizing eyes. He'd aged a little more since she'd last seen him, maybe added a couple more pounds around his waistline, but he was the same old Gary Michowsky she knew well. Driven, cunning, and overall, one hell of a cop. But stubborn as a mule.

"Nah," he replied. "We were all called in to lend a hand with the search. But the moment I heard what they found, I knew I had to bring you in."

"And the local sheriff is okay with that?"

"More than okay. Elections are up in less than a month. The last thing he wants is an unsolved murder case to bring his numbers down. He's only got a few years left until retirement, you know. He'd gladly fork this over to Palm Beach if he could."

She chuckled. "Yeah, like that's going to happen."

"Right," Michowsky replied.

"So, talk to me. Why am I here?"

"Remember a few years ago, when you told me you only needed one victim to see that it was the work of a serial killer?"

She nodded. "Sometimes you can see the signs of that psychopathology from the first victim who is found. It's apparent in the manner of death, in the killer's ritual. But usually, there are more than one. We rarely have the luck to catch serial killers before they kill for the second time. If we only have one, it means we haven't found the others yet."

Michowsky scratched his buzz-cut hair. "Well, I believe this vic fits the bill."

"Have you seen the body?" Tess asked, seeing how the

stretcher was being unloaded from the Coast Guard vessel, a forty-five-foot lifeboat. "When?"

"They heloed us over to the site, a hundred and fifty miles out," he replied.

"And CGIS didn't claim jurisdiction either?" she asked, furrowing her brow. Last thing she needed was a territorial fight with the Coast Guard Investigative Service or another agency. That would go extremely well with her boss, Special Agent in Charge Pearson.

"No," Michowsky replied calmly. "I made a strong argument, and they agreed to hand it over to you. And me, by association," he added, with a trace of excitement in his voice.

She laughed quietly, her eyes still riveted to the stretcher that was being slowly carried to shore on the shoulders of several Coasties. "What was that argument, if I may ask?"

"That they're not equipped to handle this case. I presumed they've never seen a case like this, and they had to agree."

Doc Rizza had reached dry land and directed the men to set the stretcher on the sand, a few feet from where the gentle waves washed ashore.

She started walking toward Doc Rizza, and Michowsky followed. "What are they still looking for?" Tess asked, pointing at the Coast Guard helicopters, barely visible in the distance.

"Any witness, anyone who could've seen or heard anything."

"And those two found the body, I'm assuming?" she asked, shifting her gaze toward the yacht. "Wait, don't tell me, their dog barked at something in the water?"

"Exactly," Michowsky replied. "The woman unloaded her lunch the moment she saw the floater."

"She contaminated whatever evidence was left?"

He nodded. "Yup. Barfed all over the vic."

"Great . . . just great. How far out there were they?"

"One hundred and fifty-two miles, due west."

"That far, huh?"

She kneeled next to the stretcher and greeted Doc Rizza with a quick smile. If time had been merciless with anyone in the past few months, that was the coroner. She knew he'd been struggling since his wife had passed, choosing to spend his nights at the morgue instead of his empty house, and opting for liquids instead of solids for dinner. She found herself staring at him for a good couple of seconds while making a mental note to visit him one day when they were not on a case.

"They called you, huh?" Rizza asked. "The moment I saw the body, I thought they should."

He slowly unzipped the black body bag, careful not to disturb whatever trace of evidence might still have lingered on the body. Water, especially salt water, is a great forensic countermeasure, washing most bodies clean of all trace evidence in only minutes.

Doc Rizza finished unzipping the bag and opened it. Tess approached the girl's body, focusing on her face. She hadn't been in the water too long; the bloating that irreversibly disfigures submerged bodies had not yet started to show.

Tess used a gloved finger to gently remove wet strands of hair clinging to the girl's face. Her beauty still showed, despite the bruising on her jaw and a swollen left eye. Her lips were slightly parted and pale, the lower lip a little swollen and showing some indentations and a deep split.

"What are these?" Tess asked. "Bite marks?"

"I'm going to say yes, although I will need to confirm it back at the lab." Doc Rizza sighed. "See this split, here? I'll go out on a limb and say she was hit across the face and that busted her lip, but then she was bitten hard, multiple times. Some of the bites broke her skin. See here?"

Tess didn't reply. She stared at the girl's arms, apparently tied behind her back. But something else had caught her attention.

Every bone in her naked body seemed to have been broken or crushed in multiple places. As Doc Rizza cut the cable tie that held her wrists together, her arms settled in unnatural positions. Her legs were the same, bones broken but no visible bruising. Where her wrists had been bound, deep lacerations stood in testimony of her struggle to escape, to survive.

"Any signs of sexual assault?" she asked, lowering her voice as if the media sharks could hear her from the edge of the perimeter.

He nodded. "It's a strong possibility, from what I can tell without having her on my table."

"How long has she been dead, Doc?"

"I'd say no more than three to five hours. The Gulf waters are warm and have delayed the onset of rigor, but I'm also not seeing major signs of wildlife activity on her body. Usually, fish and birds go to work after the skin has started to decay. But there are cutaneous changes of immersion present." He looked at her and added a clarification. "Her extremities are pruned."

"Can you give me a cause of death?"

"She shows signs of strangulation and the associated petechiae," he said, pointing at some bruises on her neck. "She didn't drown, I'm certain of it," he replied. "She was floating shortly after death, meaning that it wasn't the decomp gases that held her body to the surface; it's too early for those. It was the air in her lungs. We were lucky to find her. A few more hours and she would've dropped to the bottom."

"Why?"

"She was found face down, which trapped the air in her lungs and prevented it from being replaced with water. A stronger wave to flip her face up or just the passing of time would've allowed enough air to escape and her body to lose its buoyancy until decomp gases would've brought it back to the surface again."

"I see," Tess replied, "but I'll need more. What killed her, Doc?"

He sighed heavily, straightening his back with his left hand propped against his side.

"If I were to venture a guess, which I never like to do, is that she fell from high altitude. See all these broken bones? That happens when you hit the water at high velocity. It's like hitting concrete, only without the skin lacerations that come with the rough surface abrasions. I've seen this type of trauma in high-speed water-skiers."

"Yet, you're assuming she fell from up high?" Michowsky asked. He'd kept quiet for a while, a permanent frown digging ridges on his forehead.

"Yes, I'll venture a guess that she wasn't water-skiing naked with her hands tied behind her back," Doc Rizza replied.

"That's not what I meant," Michowsky said, sounding a little flustered. "I'm not an idiot. I was thinking she could've been thrown from a high-speed boat. Some of these multiengine types can easily go seventy knots."

"Got your point," Rizza replied. "I'll clarify that after I examine the fracture lines. Dropping from above doesn't have the same twisting effect that being thrown from a fast-moving vessel would have. Think of stone skipping. If thrown from a boat, her momentum versus the water surface would show in the manner her bones broke. I'll let you know."

"So, if you were to venture a time of death, Doc?" Tess asked, knowing how much the coroner hated making imprecise statements. He'd mentioned three to five hours earlier, but she wanted to confirm.

"I'd have to say it was sometime between eleven A.M. and two P.M. today. I'll know more after I finish the autopsy."

Tess peeled off her gloves and shoved her hands deep inside her pockets. She stared at the vastness of the Gulf of Mexico, wondering through what miracle the girl's body had been found.

The odds of that happening were nonexistent.

The killer had made sure of that.

3

MARRIED

At twenty-three, Richard thought the world was his. He was the single heir of a billion-dollar industrial conglomerate. He was tall and ruggedly handsome, and he was charismatic. The sports cars he loved to drive, in total disrespect for posted speed limits, were additional girl magnets, but he proved to be hard to get, although many coeds had tried and failed. For some obscure reason, it wasn't that easy to get into Richard Sanford's bed, not even in his silver Porsche.

Drawn to his good looks and his family fortune like moths to the flame, many girls attempted the impossible. Some even ignited a glint of interest in the young man's eyes, but he always chose to walk or drive away on his own. Few had noticed the clenched fists and tensed jaws when he did so. Yes, he could have them all if he wanted, but it wasn't smart to give in to his urges. And he had the willpower not to light the fire he knew he couldn't control once it was kindled.

Nonetheless, life was good for him.

He'd just graduated cum laude from Yale School of Engineering and Applied Science, and his hard-to-please father had thrown a relatively decent party for the occasion, complete with a couple of girls who didn't say no to anything he demanded, to compensate for the many times he'd refused the advances of his coeds. Come midnight on that day, his father had presented him with a formal job offer delivered pompously in a wax-sealed, gold-lettered envelope.

He was to join Sanford Industries as the vice president of

sales, on a direct path to someday taking over the reins of the company from his aging father.

Yeah, the bastard was aging all right, but not nearly fast enough. He had stamina and drive and was relentless about the business, about every minute of Richard's time. He expected Richard to give his everything to the family business, just as he had.

And so, one day, Richard came home to find his perfectly architected world was about to change.

The old man was seated in front of the study fireplace, sipping twenty-year-old scotch from a cut crystal glass and wearing cigar smoke like a halo around his balding head. On the opposite chair, a somewhat older, heavier, and more obnoxious version of his father sat with his legs crossed and a greedy grin on his face. The two men could've been brothers.

"Richard," his father had said, "have you met Mr. Wilkes?"

He promptly approached the guest and shook the hand that was offered, ignoring the cigar ash the bastard sprinkled on his shoes.

"Of Wilkes Consortium?" Richard replied with a wide smile that managed to look sincere. "No, I haven't had the pleasure yet."

That's how his slavery had started, with a stranger in his father's study, the stench of Cohibas, and a handshake he'd never forget because it had sealed his fate. He still remembered that night, the sense of uneasiness he had experienced seeing how his father fawned over Wilkes and knowing he wasn't privy to the whole story. What were the two tycoons up to?

That story started unfolding shortly thereafter. In a private conversation happening behind closed doors, his father, with an unyielding stance and a firm tone of voice, had announced

Richard's engagement to Wilkes's daughter at the same time he informed his son about his intention to merge the two companies into Sanford Wilkes Enterprises. "It makes sense," he said, blocking his son's objections with a hand gesture and a raised baritone. "We're the biggest heavy equipment manufacturer; Wilkes is number one in steel. Times have been hard while you've been partying at Yale. Not just for us, you know. All American manufacturers struggle."

"But, Dad—"

"There are no buts here. Your wedding date should be sometime before August. Now, go see your future bride. Her family is expecting us on Sunday for the official proposal of marriage. Just a small circle of friends, nothing big. About two hundred people or so."

"Dad—" he tried to plead, but he couldn't get a word in.

"Not another word, son," the old man said, letting himself fall heavy in his burgundy leather armchair. He looked older all of a sudden, tired, drawn.

Richard crouched in front of his chair to be on the same eye level. "What's going on, Dad?"

The old man sighed and lit another cigar. "We need this to happen. Our cash flow's been taking a beating for years now. We have become dependent on steel imports at high prices. If we want to survive, if you want your legacy to be worth more than a pile of junk, we need this alliance to take place and be sealed with more than signatures on a contract."

He found himself at a loss for words. He wanted to swear, scream, strangle the old man with his bare hands. After all, mergers could be signed without having to marry someone. That was so last century.

"She's not that bad, son," his father added, as if reading his mind. "You don't have to love her." He blew a cloud of bluish smoke in the air, sending it twirling above Richard's head. "She's totally fuckable, you know? I'd marry her myself if her old man would allow it," the old man added with a raspy, lewd laugh that morphed into a coughing spell.

Maybe Geneva Wilkes *looked* fuckable, but was she, really? Richard's needs were special, leaving him with little choice but to seek the company of women who were willing to satisfy his intense urges without objections.

The moment he'd seen Geneva, he knew those urges were to be denied, confined to the darkest recesses of his lusting body when he shared the bed of his wife, kept under the strictest control. The classy, snobby socialite, who hadn't even agreed to take his name, was an ice block in bed. She probably had the same enthusiasm for their union as he had. Noticing that, he was relieved to see he could visit with her less and less often, and she voiced no complaints, apparently, preferring to sleep with her Löwchen dog Althea than with him. Even the dog was a pretentious little snob; apparently only a few remained in the world and had been the dogs of choice for Chinese emperors, at some point or another in their spoiled history. The mutt looked like a regular, fluffy canine accessory to him anyway, and Geneva could've gotten a dog looking just like that from the local pound.

But that pretentious furball and his wife's low libido had brought him the freedom to spend his nights at will, as long as he was discreet about it. And that he was. He'd learned the need for discretion the hard way.

Their marriage evolved well in the first couple of years, if what they had could even be called a marriage. But one night, after an exquisite meal and a certain bottle of Pineau des

Charentes, a sweet French wine with unexpected consequences, he made a drunken pass at his wife, and she didn't send him away. Maybe she was just as horny as he was, after sipping two glasses of that intoxicating elixir. They held hands all the way back from the Palme d'Or restaurant in Coral Gables, and they almost tore each other's clothes before reaching the bedroom door.

Lust and wine swirled in his heated body, fueled by Geneva's eager moans and undulating body, and soon he forgot all about his need to control his urges. Overtaken by dark passion, he tied her hands and smothered her screams until he found his release. He hadn't noticed that halfway through his assault, she'd stopped fighting him, choosing to stare at him with cold eyes, waiting for it to be over, the determination in her gaze as steeled as her family's roots.

Lying spent and grateful by her side, Richard had removed her restraints and placed a kiss on her cold lips. "Baby, you were amazing," he'd whispered, still oblivious to her deathly stare.

She got up and wrapped a silk robe around her body, then rubbed her sore wrists for a long minute, staring at the naked man lying in her bed. Then she turned away and left without a word.

The following day, she was waiting for him in the living room when he came home. Seeing her icy glare, his smile died on his lips while worry unfurled in his gut, setting off alarm bells.

"I knew who you were before we were married," she said, going straight to the point without any introduction. "You don't think I was going to marry a total stranger without a full background check, did you?"

She waited for him to reply, but he stood frozen, slack-jawed.

"Baby, what are you talking about?" he managed to ask, but his voice was trembling pitifully.

"You gave me some nice souvenirs last night," she added, showing her bruised wrists. "But don't worry, my dear," she added, her voice dipped in poison. "These will heal. That's why I have taken photos of every bruise you left on my body and placed them in safekeeping with my lawyer, in case some unforeseen accident would happen, and I'd be hurt in any way."

He swallowed hard, as he started to comprehend where this was going.

"Now, let's discuss the new terms of our marriage, my dear husband."

She paused again, expecting him to agree. All he could do was nod, his teeth too clenched to allow any spoken words to come out.

"I'll keep it simple. You do what I say, when I say, how I say. That includes everything, even sex. You are not to lay a single finger on me without permission, ever again." She smiled, seemingly savoring his humiliation and prolonging it. "If you break this arrangement, the photos will come out, and with them, the entire dossier my investigator put together on your youthful indiscretions."

A jolt of fear traveled through his body. How much did she know?

"Yes, that dossier includes the girls you raped at Yale. Remember those poor creatures? Did you know one of them needed hospitalization? Did you even care? How much did your daddy fork out to make them go away?"

She stood and then picked up her fluffy mutt, quickly placing a smooch on the dog's nose with a smile and a happy flicker of love in her gaze. Then she faced him, her eyes turned steel-cold again.

"Welcome to your new life, hubby dear. May it be a long and painful one. If you had any self-esteem, you'd shoot yourself."

Minutes after she'd left and closed the door, his jaws were still clenched so badly he didn't feel the pain from the molar he'd cracked while grinding his teeth to keep himself from killing her right where she'd stood.

He was screwed for life. The damn bitch from hell would never let him go.

But one day he'd be free.

Like *Mile High Death*?

Buy it now!

Preview: *A Beautiful Couple*

LESLIE WOLFE

Her husband
killed someone.

She's the
only witness.

A
BEAUTIFUL
COUPLE

1

AMANDA DAVIS

I killed a man.

The surreal words fill my mind, echoing in shock and fear with tremors that weaken my body. As reality starts setting in, I gasp silently, covering my mouth with a trembling hand, stifling a sob. Wide-eyed, I stare at the body lying in a motionless heap at the bottom of the stairs, disbelief clinging to me in scattered thoughts and anxious breaths.

It can't be true. He can't be dead.

But I can see it's all too real. In his neck, twisted and crooked sideways in an impossible posture. In the sickening crack of broken bones I remember hearing just as he was landing on the hardwood floor after bouncing down the steep flight of stairs. In the pooling blood that's slowly seeping from his head, gleaming burgundy under the yellowish light coming from the floor lamp by the door.

A noise outside makes me jump out of my skin. Someone's coming. I freeze in place at the top of the stairs, my fingers white-knuckled on the handrail, as the footsteps draw closer. Then, in the dark frame of the living room window, the profile of a woman appears, her face dimly lit as she passes by. Without turning her head to look inside.

I breathe.

Then I realize someone could've seen what happened. A passerby. A neighbor. Anyone.

I force some air into my lungs to steel my fraught nerves. Still holding on to the handrail for support, I climb down the stairs, careful not to slip, as if his fall could repeat somehow and seal my fate in vengeful symmetry, my body next to his. I hold my breath as I approach, senselessly hoping he's still alive, yet fearing it. When I eventually breathe, the metallic smell of blood fills my nostrils, filling me with dread.

I rush to the window and close the blinds, then peek outside between two slats. The street is eerily deserted and still. For now.

Crouching by his side, I feel for a pulse with frozen fingers. Touching his skin sears me, prickling the back of my head as if he could snap out of death and grab my shaky wrist.

There's no pulse.

His golf shirt is soaked with blood at the collar and smells faintly of aftershave, although his face shows a two-day stubble. His skull is fractured where it must've hit the edge of a step, the indentation clearly visible through his buzz-cut hair despite the bleeding laceration. Reluctantly, I slip my fingers and trace his neck, wincing as I find the protruding vertebra, a sign of a fractured cervical spine resulting in a fatal spinal cord injury.

He died the moment he hit the floor.

I'm more than qualified to make that statement. It doesn't change how I feel, though. Unsure of myself. Scared. Unsteady. My heart is racing, and my chest is tightening, as if the walls of this room are drawing closer and closer, about to squeeze the life out of me.

The sound of an approaching car makes me rush to the window and peek outside. It doesn't slow down until it reaches the corner and turns, tinting the darkness with hues of bright taillight red.

I turn on my heels and stare at the body, unsure what to do.

His eyes are still open, as if looking straight through me with hypnotizing, dilated pupils. It chills the blood in my veins. Barely touching him with the tips of my fingers, I crouch down and close his eyelids swiftly, shaking, eager to put some distance between me and him. I stand quickly and step back, feeling for the handrail, unable to take my eyes off of him. Part of me still expects him to get up and grab me, slam me against the wall, then put his hands around my throat and squeeze until my world goes dark. Just as his is now.

But he doesn't move. He's dead.

I killed him.

The enormity of what I've done weighs heavily on my heart. How could I let this happen?

It seems I had no choice, and yet, the truth is I *had* a choice, and I made the wrong one. That didn't happen a few moments ago, when I pushed him down the stairs.

No.

It happened earlier. Much earlier.

And now, I have to deal with the consequences of what I've done.

My first thought is to run, to put as much distance as I possibly can between me and the body lying on the blood-soaked floor. But there's no running away from this. Not right now. Not without a plan.

Still walking backward, my heel stops against the bottom step of the staircase and I nearly trip. I let myself slide down and sit on a step. For a moment of respite, my elbows rest on my shaky knees and my face lands in my hands, hiding from the grim sight.

Perhaps I could stall things for a few days before they come for me, because I know they will. Clinging to that glimmer of hope, my mind starts working. I raise my weary head and look around, taking inventory of everything I could use to buy myself some time. There isn't much.

One thing's certain: I have to get rid of the body.

That's when I realize I need help.

He's massive, at least six-three and well-built, weighing perhaps two-forty or about that much. It's what I liked about him... the strength, the agility, the apparent stamina and self-confidence. However, I'm not nearly that tall, and I'm one-forty at the most, on a bad, bloated day. I reach for his leg to test my strength, but stop before touching his ankle. It's pointless to even try. At work, it takes six of us to transfer a patient his size from the stretcher onto the bed.

I take out my phone and turn it on. The bitten apple lights up white on the black screen, then vanishes, making room for a picture of my son. Tristan just turned nine; we took that pic last summer, on the Santa Monica Pier. Seeing his piercing blue eyes touched by his enchanted smile brings the threat of tears to my eyes.

What if I lose him? What if they lock me up and I never see him again?

I can't bear the thought of that; it guts me. *No... I can't lose my son. It won't happen. Whatever it takes.*

I push the grim thoughts away and breathe deeply while putting in the passcode. His face disappears off the screen.

It will be all right. But the words I tell myself fail to reassure me.

As the screen fills with apps, I realize there's only one person I can call for the kind of help I need. The one person I'd rather never call or see again. My fingers falter retrieving the name from the contacts list. Hesitating, I give the fallen body another look, desperately wondering if there's any other way.

There isn't.

I brace myself for the questions that are about to come my way like machine gun bullets, merciless and cold and ripping through me in rapid-fire sequence.

Then I make the call, knowing that as soon as I share what I've done, there will be no turning back. My entire existence will be at the mercy of someone else. Someone I know I can't trust.

As the line rings in my ear, I reflect bitterly on the last few weeks, on everything that's happened.

I never wanted any of this.

All I wanted was a stupid divorce.

2

PAUL DAVIS

Two weeks ago

Hot damn. Tits like those should be illegal.

I touch my tie knot briefly, wishing I could loosen it a little. Instead, I end up straightening it—a reflex when I know I'm directly in camera view. Only, there's no camera trained on me. Not yet.

The cameras are all huddled outside the ballroom, where the guests keep arriving in their fancy cars and rental limos to attend the annual *Citizens Against Impaired Driving* fundraiser I'm chairing. Even so, I should be focusing on the people seated at the table with me, including my wife Amanda. But no...I can't focus on any of them.

Only on her, the stranger who captured my interest the moment we arrived at the venue. She's walking across the atrium with a sway of her hips, so rhythmic and smooth that it's as if she's dancing her way through to the light music in the background. Her satin gown hugs her perfect shape, taut over her perky, little breasts. A high leg slit lets me put eyes on more of her skin than my wife would appreciate. Good thing Amanda's not looking at me right now. She's chatting with an older woman seated next to her while I get to feast my eyes on the unsuspecting stranger.

The woman doesn't look my way, and I'm not used to being ignored. To feeling invisible. I hate how it makes me feel. I almost want to shout, "Hey, I'm here," but there's no point. I'd make an ass of myself. As she makes her way to the open bar, she turns away, and I can see that gown is a backless wonder, seemingly clinging only to her shoulders...and so lightly, I could make it fall off of her with the touch of a finger. The thought unsettles me. I shift in my seat. And keep watching.

Her back is just as perfect as everything else she's strutting. The dress, a deep shade of red, shimmers under the dim lights, generously draped and still tight over her ass. It dips daringly below the small of her flawless back. I can't keep my eyes off her.

I bet she's not wearing anything underneath that thing. For a moment, I imagine how it would feel to touch her smooth, glowing skin. How that perfectly shaped back would arch when I took her from behind. How she'd look at me after, laying spent on crumpled sheets, with her wavy, chestnut hair spread on my pillow.

She disappears from sight as a couple of men trail after her and block my view. They're probably sucked in by her wake, empty drink glasses in hand and following her like panting dogs on the prowl. I'm about to down my drink and give myself a reason to visit the open bar where she's headed, but my glass freezes in mid-air when I notice Amanda's eyes, drilling into me with barely contained rage.

She leans toward me until her breath touches my skin. "Really, Paul?" she whispers in my ear, faking a smile for whoever might be looking at us just now. "With me here? With all these people watching?"

My teeth grit as I set my glass down. I hate being scolded like I'm four. "I didn't do anything," I growl back in a low voice, hating myself for saying it, for making excuses. She doesn't reply. Just sits there smiling, pretending everything is okay, but her chest is heaving, and her lower lip is trembling slightly.

But I'm still angry.

I'll admit I can get pissed off easily.

I take a sip of bourbon to hide the emotion, and pretend to pay some attention to what an overly bejeweled, middle-aged woman across the ten-person table is telling me. But it's pointless; I'm too frustrated to care. She goes on and on about a nephew of hers who died, and I'm forced to sit here, nod, and take it. She makes sweet eyes at me, and I fear I'll be throwing up in my mouth soon. I wash away the bad taste with more bourbon, then continue to smile and nod every now and then as she tells her endless story. Soon enough, she'll write me a check.

That's why I'm here, for the *Citizens Against Impaired Driving* annual fundraiser, gracefully hosted in the university atrium. The vast room is lavishly decorated with cascading white flowers set on every ten-person table, placed at the center of fine, white table linen. We're seated on dressed-up chairs tied up with satin ribbons. The myriad lights are dimly shining above us from chandelier-like, modern LED fixtures featuring intricate layers of crystal-clear prisms that glimmer in flickers of rainbow. These are not the drab, fluorescent university atrium lights I remember from my prior visits. They must've had them replaced for tonight. They really went over the top this time. I'm impressed.

The sound of my wife's laughter catches my attention. She looks beautiful tonight, with her long, blond hair done perfectly so, and she captures the undivided attention of at least two men. And I'm supposed to be okay with that. As if she can read my mind, her hand lands on my forearm. I pull away, instinctively, the thought of being seen as my wife's attachment bothering me on a deep level.

The air hums with low-key chatter and the occasional drunken burst of laughter. Because, of course, what's more fitting for a sobriety organization event than an open bar?

The event is sponsored generously and advertised for free by Golden State Broadcasting, the TV station I work for. They make sure that all invitation-only attendees can afford to fork out at least a couple grand for the four-course gourmet meal and said open bar. And the privilege to mingle with television people and the few Hollywood stars in attendance, and perhaps get a selfie with someone famous.

And as the president of *Citizens Against Impaired Driving* for the past few years, I'm at the center of all of it, soon to take the stage for the final speech of the evening, as soon as the guests finish their desserts.

Yet, I'm annoyed as fuck.

My boss, Raymond Cook, the president and CEO of Golden State Broadcasting, is a balding bundle of blundering ego. This year, the fourth in the pained history of his favorite event, he decided that the most prominent people in the station be seated with random donors, to engage them in conversation and have them imbibing and star-struck by the time they sign those checks. For what it's worth, he was fair; he's seated with donors, too. But he doesn't have unfuckable women drooling all over him while his wife is seated by his side. And that's not because he's not married. It's because no one really knows who Raymond Cook is. And no one cares.

But Paul Davis? That's a different story.

3

PAUL DAVIS

I'm the face of the evening news and the brains behind it. I'm the lead anchor, and there's a reason for that. On the evenings I'm working, the Nielsen ratings go up, ad revenue climbs by at least ten percent, and viewership and engagement both spike. Yes, I'll admit that the spike is mostly reflecting women, and I'm secretly pleased with it.

With ratings like that, I got my own show two years ago. It's a fifteen-minute interview attached to the end of the news program, called *The Final Question*. There's no co-anchor involved; just me and whomever I choose—carefully—to skewer or commend that evening, dealer's choice. The show's been quite successful, further increasing the station's ratings. That's why Raymond Cook decided I should report directly to him. It was an actual promotion and came with more money— lots more money. Unfortunately, it also came with a closer working relationship between Raymond and me.

I'm not that happy about that part.

I hate his guts, and I'm sure he envies my popularity, although his bottom line loves it. Regardless of how I might feel about it, though, he's still the boss. He gets to call the shots. All of them. And never lets me forget it.

But that's not the only fly in my bourbon.

My former co-anchor, Carly Crown, is seated at my right. She's stunningly elegant in a sapphire blue dress with a plunging neckline that draws the immediate attention of every male in the room. Some females, too. Her blond hair is styled in loose waves and, tonight, looks disturbingly like my wife's. Perhaps she didn't intend it to, but I wouldn't put it past her. Every now and then, her knee rubs against my thigh.

I usually like the seemingly casual interactions, the not-so-accidental touching, the innuendo coloring our conversations at work. But not tonight. Not with a pissed off Amanda seated at my left. I don't want trouble on the home front.

Pulling away, I shoot Carly a warning glance. She veers her eyes toward the empty stage, but there's a certain tension in her lips that tells me I'm going to hear about my distance real soon. And I'm not going to like it. Carly is a death hazard dressed in Pierre Cardin.

The woman across the table stops speaking mid-phrase as the lights in the atrium grow brighter. Raymond climbs onto the stage and grabs the microphone. The light music in the background fades. He clears his voice and coughs into his fist—thankfully, before the mic goes live.

"Thank you all for being here with us tonight in beautiful Malibu. What a fantastic setting for such a noble cause! I hope you enjoyed the delicious meal as much as I did—though I must admit, the dessert might've been a bit too good. If I don't fit into my tux tomorrow, I'll know who to blame!"

The room regales him with a roar of laughter. I can tell the open bar made a difference this year.

"But before the evening comes to an end, there's the moment you've all been waiting for." He pauses for a moment, and the audience stills.

About fucking time.

We've been doing this for four years, and this is the first time he's letting me speak. I straighten my tie knot once more, but refrain from smoothing my hair with my hands. I'm ready.

No, I'm not. I take another sip of bourbon. *Now, I am.*

"She saves lives for a living," Raymond says, gesturing at and looking in Amanda's direction. The limelight follows his lead and finds us. My wife smiles shyly and bows her head. "As a critical care nurse working the endless battlefields of impaired driving, she's the first one to see the carnage. She will tell you that not everyone makes it, even if Sunset Valley Medical Center's Trauma Unit is one of the best in the nation. She has witnessed, time and again, the heartbreak a split-second bad decision can bring upon families."

He pauses for a moment, then shifts his focus to me. "He is a trusted voice in our community, bringing us the news with integrity and dedication. You know him well; you welcome him into your homes at dinnertime. And before you turn on the news to hear of yet another tragedy that has bloodied the streets of Los Angeles, he hears of it first. He investigates, uncovers the truth, and delivers it to you with all of the shocking details." It's my turn to smile and nod in acknowledgement. "Together, they are a beautiful couple, partnering to play a pivotal role in our organization's success and drive critical change in legislation, with your help. Please welcome Amanda and Paul Davis, ladies and gentlemen!"

My wife and I stand as the audience starts applauding. Beaming, Carly chooses that moment to step up into our limelight and hug me, as if we're at the Oscars or something. She lingers in the hug, filling my nostrils with her scent, grinding her hip against me. I pull away discreetly, knowing all cameras are trained on us. Then, I offer Amanda an arm that she quickly takes as we walk toward the makeshift stage.

She stands by my side at the lectern when I take the mic. The crowd quiets down looking at me, and I love it. "Thank you all for being here tonight. Before we get into the serious stuff, I wanted to share a little joke I heard recently: Why did the reporter sit on the teleprompter?" A pause for effect. "Because they wanted to stay on top of the news!"

The audience laughs heartily, and I bask in it. Then, as the response subsides, I continue. "Alright, now that we've had a laugh, let me tell you a story." I look at my wife, and she nods almost imperceptibly. "About how we started *Citizens Against Impaired Driving*, and, most of all, why. It was when we both realized that our jobs had too much death in them. For Amanda, it was the lives that the amazing team at Sunset Valley couldn't save. Senseless deaths that could've been avoided. For me, it was the litany of incidents I had to bring to you via the news I delivered, every single night. Not a day of respite in our lives and yours; not a day of not having to talk about yet another horrifying 'accident' happening here in LA." I allow a beat of silence to pass so my message can sink in. "It just has to stop. And you can make it happen. *We* can make it happen. Together."

As I say those words, the last of them being drowned by enthusiastic applause, my throat scorches for a drink. At a table close to the podium, the beauty in the backless red dress smiles at me.

I make eye contact and hold it for a moment. Her smile blooms, her head tilting slightly as she throws me a loaded look.

For a moment, I forget about Amanda.

Who knows what the evening might still bring? It's looking good for now.

Like *A Beautiful Couple?*

LESLIE WOLFE

Her husband
killed someone.

She's the
only witness.

A
BEAUTIFUL
COUPLE

Buy it now!

ABOUT THE AUTHOR

Meet Leslie Wolfe, bestselling author and mastermind behind gripping thrillers that have won the hearts of over three million readers worldwide. She brings a fresh and invigorating touch to the thriller genre, crafting compelling narratives around unforgettable, powerhouse women.

You might know her from the Detective Kay Sharp series or have been hooked by Tess Winnett's relentless pursuit of justice. Maybe you've followed the dynamic duo Baxter & Holt through the gritty streets of Las Vegas or plunged into political intrigue with Alex Hoffmann.

Recently, Leslie published *The Girl You Killed*, a psychological thriller that's pure, unputdownable suspense. This standalone novel will have fans of *The Undoing*, *The Silent Patient*, and *Little Fires Everywhere* on the edge of their seats.

Whether you're into the mind games of *Criminal Minds*, love crime thrillers like James Patterson's, or enjoy the heart-pounding tension in Kendra Elliot and Robert Dugoni's mysteries, Leslie's got a thriller series for you. Fans of action-packed writers like Tom Clancy or Lee Child will find plenty to love in her Alex Hoffmann series.

Wolfe's latest psychological thriller, *A Beautiful Couple*, will have you racing through the pages gasping for breath until the final jaw-dropping twist, delighting fans of *Gone Girl* and *The Girl on the Train*.

Discover all of Leslie's works on Amazon.com/LeslieWolfe. Want a sneak peek at what's next? Become an insider for early access to previews of her new novels, each a thrilling ride you won't want to miss.

BOOKS BY LESLIE WOLFE

STANDALONE TITLES

A Beautiful Couple
The Surgeon
The Girl You Killed
The Hospital
If I Go Missing
Stories Untold
Love, Lies and Murder

TESS WINNETT SERIES

Dawn Girl
The Watson Girl
Glimpse of Death
Taker of Lives
Not Really Dead
Girl With A Rose
Mile High Death
The Girl They Took
The Girl Hunter

DETECTIVE KAY SHARP SERIES

The Girl From Silent Lake
Beneath Blackwater River
The Angel Creek Girls
The Girl on Wildfire Ridge
Missing Girl at Frozen Falls

BAXTER & HOLT SERIES

Las Vegas Girl
Casino Girl
Las Vegas Crime

ALEX HOFFMANN SERIES

Executive
Devil's Move
The Backup Asset
The Ghost Pattern
Operation Sunset

For the complete list of books in all available formats, visit:
Amazon.com/LeslieWolfe